Chasing
Temptation

a Chasing Love novel

JOYA RYAN

Entangled Publishing, LLC
2614 South Timberline Road
Suite 109
Fort Collins, CO 80525
Visit our website at www.entangledpublishing.com.

Brazen is an imprint of Entangled Publishing, LLC. For more information on our titles, visit www.brazenbooks.com.

Edited by Stephen Morgan
Cover design by Heather Howland

Manufactured in the United States of America

First Edition October 2014

To My Sister Katie
Thank you for being supportive and awesome! I love you.

Chapter One

Penny glanced down at herself. The white top she wore was tight, clung to her curves, and, with the few buttons in front undone, gave sight to some major cleavage. She'd taken her friend Lily's advice and paired the top with a short skirt and sexy heels, but now she had to wonder...

"You sure this isn't too much?"

She wiggled her toes, insecurity slowly pumping through her veins.

Lily tugged on the fabric of Penny's shirt, trying to close the buttons. "Maybe suck it in a little?"

"I can't suck in my boobs."

Lily shrugged and stepped back to look at her. "Screw it, I say leave it undone. It looks hot. Besides, it's Jenna's bachelorette party," she said, fastening her earing. "You're supposed to dress a little slutty for the club."

The club was half an hour away and the closest thing to a "night life scene" available to the people from the small town of Diamond, Kansas. Well, aside from Penny's BBQ bar and restaurant. She'd taken over the BBQ when her mother passed away last year. The long hours hadn't left much time for her to have fun. She didn't go to clubs, or the city for that matter, but that didn't mean she didn't like fun…wasn't open to new things.

The last time she'd attempted to try "new things" was in the bedroom with her ex-boyfriend. Eli was courteous, handsome, all things a gentleman should be. He'd even been patient with Penny when she made him wait six months before finally having sex.

The sex had been a wild disappointment, so a week later she'd put on her best lingerie and gone to surprise him with round two. What she discovered was that he'd already found his own round two, and it wasn't with her. Soon after taking her virginity, he'd taken her dignity by cheating on her with someone more "sexy" than "adorably boring."

His words still rang in her ears:

"You're just too vanilla, Penny."

That had stung, coming from a guy that color-coded his sock drawer, and she'd never quite come out of the shadow he'd cast over her self-esteem. She'd discovered there was a wild side to her waiting to be unleashed, but the first time she'd tried to let out her inner sex kitten, he'd dumped her.

Which was why her sexual experience was lacking. That one time with Eli was her *only* experience. She'd thought about dating again, even gotten a few admiring glances, but her older brother Ryder did a great job keeping the male population of Diamond far away from her. And she was tired of it. Especially since she'd just found out that Eli was coming back into town with his new fiancé. AKA the other woman.

Diamond was too small a town for her not to run into him. If—when—she saw him, she wanted to know for herself that he wouldn't wreck her.

"Besides," Lily said, "this is the kind of outfit you need to catch the kind of man you're fishing for."

Penny swallowed hard. Funny Lily had phrased it that way, because she was going *fishing*, and Penny had her eyes on a big *Bass*. As in Sebastian "Bass" Strafford. The one man she'd had a secret crush on for years. He was dark, brooding, and a bad ass attorney, who also happened to be her older brother's best friend.

"Ryder's going to wet himself if he sees me dressed like this," Penny said.

Jenna and Colt McCade had been engaged since last summer, and their spring wedding was right around the corner. Thanks to her friends being disgustingly in love, they'd decided to thrown a joint bachelor-bachelorette party at the club. Which meant Penny's brother Ryder would be there.

But so would Bass. And that made tonight the perfect chance for Penny to make her move. She not only trusted him—they'd been friends for years, after all—she knew he was the kind of man that could deliver in the bedroom. Just looking at him was enough to know that.

Not to mention the few whispers she'd heard over the years about Bass being some kind of "sex god." And that made him perfect for her. Who better to teach her how to be a sex goddess than a god himself?

"You might have to help me distract Ryder," she said.

"He'll have to get over himself. You're a grown ass woman. This is your chance," Lily said, cupping Penny's shoulders. Lily's blond hair was fastened into a tight up-do, and the trademark McCade flare was prominent. "Time to implement Operation: Orgasm."

Penny needed some of Lily's confidence. "What if I get shot down?"

"If a guy shoots you down, he's a moron," Lily said. "There's going to be a lot of hot guys, ones more than willing to show you a good time. And sex is a good thing. As long as you're comfortable and feel good about it, there's no reason not to go after what you want."

Problem was, who she wanted was her brother's best friend, a fact Bass wouldn't overlook lightly. She would have to be persuasive if she was going to get the rigid attorney to bend to her idea.

Whatever the end result would be, going for Sebastian tonight was putting the group dynamic in jeopardy. But she had to try.

She knew he was attracted to her. At least, she thought she knew. Last year they'd played a harmless game of Sardines that turned into a few minutes of Sebastian lying against her in the dark, and her breathing in his scent.

She'd thought for sure he was going to kiss her. He'd been close. She could still feel his breath against her lips when he'd whispered the phrase she'd been repeating in her mind for nearly nine months:

Don't challenge me. I always get what I want in the end.

Usually what he wanted was short term flings. If gossip was to be believed, those flings were full of the wildest sex a person could imagine. The thought made her tingle all over. She'd caught his attention, got a glimpse at the man he was hiding underneath, and was now determined to experience what lay behind that domineering persona.

"I'm going for it," Penny said. She gave her long red hair a flick and faced her friend. "Time for Operation: Orgasm to commence."

. . .

Bass glanced at the brunette across the room. She'd been checking him out for the past ten minutes. She was attractive, and that smile she gave was one he recognized. A look that led to the bedroom.

"If that woman keeps staring at you like that, her panties are going to catch fire," Huck Galvin said loudly into Sebastian's ear over the booming music of the club.

Yeah, that brunette could end his dry spell. She was prime, ready, and most importantly, *not* Penny Diamond.

Get her out of your head.

Good fucking luck with that. He'd been trying to get her out of his mind ever since last summer when they'd played Sardines. He'd always thought she was too soft for him, but after she'd challenged him to a game where he ended up alone with her, he'd barely been able to resist tasting those lush lips of hers. He could still feel her body humming against his, begging for it.

She was everything bright and good. He'd known her a long time, and he'd never met her equal. And he'd looked. Hard. But no one could compare to the soul-deep genuineness of Penny Diamond.

He shook his head and focused on the brunette. That was the kind of surface woman he needed. She looked experienced and able to handle his needs in the bedroom. Needs so strong they'd evolved into a dark secret.

He loved sex, loved women, but his tastes were…not for the timid. They also weren't long term.

He'd learned at a young age that love and companionship didn't equal commitment. Sooner or later, someone got restless and moved on. Just like his mother had done when he was a kid. Just like Bass did with every "relationship" he had. Being the leaver was better than being left. Which was why he had a firm system: nothing lasted beyond two weeks. Besides, most women only wanted—or could handle—a single night with him. After they saw what he was like in bed, they were usually done. Satisfied, but overwhelmed. Which just about said it all, didn't it? Even if love and commitment were for other people, they weren't for him.

Too bad all I can think about is Penny.

No one goaded him like she did. She knew how to push his buttons and played on the very need that drove him both in and out of bed.

Control.

He swallowed down the last of his whiskey.

Stop thinking about her.

She was the last person he could ever be with. Between her overbearing older brother, who happened to be his best friend, and her innocent eyes and bright smile, she wasn't the kind of woman who would want what Sebastian dished out.

He looked around the large club, bright lights flickering amongst the darkness, people dancing, the temperature rising to hot and humid. Usually in a suit, he was happy for the weekends when he got to wear a T-shirt and jeans.

"I thought this was your scene, Bassy?" Colt said, walking up, drinks in hand. "But I could see your frownie face all the way from across the bar."

"Poor Bass is girl shy tonight," Huck said, chuckling. "I think he's PMSing."

Great, now both of his friends were giving him shit.

Though they were being dicks, they were like his brothers. Between them, having a great job that he loved and living in a town that felt like home, he was fairly happy. This past year, however, with all the love bullshit in the air wafting from Colt and Jenna, his mood had been on the pissy side. He wished the best for his friends, but their wedding planning and happily ever after gushing only reminded him that kind of thing would never be for him. No serious woman. No long term commitment. That was too much power to give someone else. Hell, his competitive nature was what made him a great attorney. He didn't lose because he had no fear. Nothing loved, nothing lost.

Ever.

His life was best spent a couple weeks at a time with clear expectations.

"You're giving me shit, and you're the one having a joint bachelor party with your fiancée," Bass said, taking the whiskey in Colt's hand, which left Bass double-fisted, whiskey in one hand, a beer in the other.

"Hey, my fiancée is the hottest thing in here." He glanced around. "Well, she will be when she gets here."

"Look at him," Huck said, laughing. "He's like a damn puppy."

"It's sad really," Bass agreed.

Colt just smiled, his stare locked on the entrance. "Ah fellas, you have no idea what you're in for once the right woman ropes you."

Colt didn't give them another word, just hustled toward

the entrance, and Bass saw why. Jenna was walking through, and right behind her was Lily and—

"Holy fucking Christ," he said, his eyes falling out of his head.

Penny Diamond strutted in behind her friends, looking all kinds of deliciously fuckable.

"Oh shit," Huck said with a wide smile, obviously looking at the same thing Bass was. "Ryder is going to piss his pants when he sees his baby sister trussed up like a—"

"Careful," Bass warned.

Huck's smile only grew. "I was going to say 'hottie.' I love Penny. I'd never say a bad word about her."

Bass knew that. They'd all been friends for a long time.

"But I had no idea little Penny was so...curvy." Huck's statement made heat rise in Sebastian's gut. A feeling like jealousy.

Yeah, *little Penny* was more than curvy. Her five-two frame was hoisted to a staggering five-six in those sinful stilettos. The scrap of fabric she called a skirt showcased tone legs, and the top she wore hugged her flat stomach and full breasts. She was built for a wet dream, had the face of an angel, ivory skin, pouty lips, red hair, and the greenest eyes ever created. And tonight, those gems glanced around until they finally landed on him.

He checked the urge to groan. She didn't look like Little Miss Diamond tonight, and she sure as hell didn't look like anyone's little sister. She looked like she was ready for every fantasy he had—fantasies she'd been the star of lately.

His phone vibrated in his pocket. He dug it out and looked. A text from Ryder.

Ryder: *Hey bro, can't make the party tonight. Got held up in Wichita. Big meeting tomorrow morning. Tell Colt sorry and keep an eye on Penny for me.*

Great, just fucking great. Ryder was his saving grace to keep his cool around Penny. But now he was charged to *keep an eye on her*? He wanted to do a lot more than just look at the sultry redhead.

"Ryder is still in Wichita," Bass said to Huck. "He's not coming at all."

"That sucks. I'll let Colt know. You coming?" Huck asked, heading toward their group of friends several tables away.

Bass shook his head. "I'm going to hang back for a few."

"Ah, gonna make a move on the brunette, huh?" Huck asked.

No, he was staying put, because if he left the table, he might get closer to Penny. Might touch her. Forget why that was a bad idea.

"Something like that."

Huck headed toward the group and sat with them at the other end of the club. Bass stayed at his table. The packed dance floor between him and Penny might be enough distance.

Except he saw with one part fear, one part hunger, that she was walking in his direction. Her breasts damn near bouncing out of her top with every stride.

He thought—hoped—she was headed his way. Her eyes were locked on him, after all. But that would be bad. Because the closer she came, the further his mind traveled to all the images of her writhing beneath him. Her skin was the color of fresh cream, and he had no doubt her ass would look amazing warmed and pink from his hand.

He'd bend her over, slap her ass while he fucked her hard. Fucked her until she begged for release. But he wouldn't give it. It would be punishment for wearing that outfit. Flaunting her body that was his to command—

No. Not mine. She's. Not. Mine.

He'd tell himself this a thousand times if he had to. And he'd hate it every single time.

Just when he thought she would saunter her sweet ass over to him, she stopped to chat up some cowboy. The prick leaned down and said something in her ear, and she smiled and tucked a lock of ruby hair behind her ear. All while she kept her eyes on Bass.

What the hell? Was she *trying* to make him jealous?

The heat that had started in his gut flamed to a full on fire and burned his blood.

He didn't know what the cowboy was saying, but judging by Penny's swaying movements and laugh, the asshole was obviously hitting on her. And the way she raised her brows in Bass's direction, as if saying, *What are you going to do about it?* He was certain now what she was trying to do to him. Shit of it was, it was working.

Bass took one step in her direction, something she seemed to notice, and those green eyes lit up.

She was playing a dangerous game. One that required him to keep his focus and control. Good thing that was his specialty. He might not be able to have her, but the cowboy asshole wasn't going to either. He'd never felt a deeper need to take her, claim her, than in that moment.

But I can't...

So he'd bury the notion and the feeling. And he'd stand

there, unmoving, simply watching with a vengeance.

Except she kept talking to the asshole. No, not talking, openly flirting. But those emerald eyes stayed on Sebastian. Brushing her hair back, she ran two fingers along her collarbone.

He clenched his teeth.

She smiled and nodded at the cowboy. He left, heading to the bar, likely getting her a drink. Penny continued her trek toward Bass.

"Penelope," he said when she reached him.

"Why are you sulking over here?"

"Not sulking." He took a drink and looked her over. Whatever she saw in his gaze made her lick her lips, spurring new fantasies about what he wanted to do with that mouth of hers. "You're making new friends I see." He gestured toward the bar where asshole cowboy was.

"Oh, that's Rob. He seems nice enough. Getting me a drink."

"I'm sure he is."

She frowned. "Is there a problem? You seem grouchy. Huck warned me you were in a mood."

Oh, he was in a mood all right. She brushed her hand along her collarbone again, and Bass had no choice but to watch and wish to hell it was him touching that sweet skin.

"I'm trying to figure out why the hell you're dressed like that."

"You don't like it?" she said, her sarcasm evident in her tone. She glanced down at herself, knowing damn well he liked her outfit. Every man in there did. "What would you dress me in then?"

"That's not my decision to make."

"What if it were?"

Whatever she knew about him, she was using it right then. She knew his love of control and how to tempt him with it. He'd dress her all right. In nothing but those heels and restraints on her wrists. He stayed silent, too afraid he might reveal his true thoughts.

"Nothing to say?" she asked. Again, he stayed quiet. "Other than you not liking my outfit, right?"

"Correct."

"I would expect better lying from an attorney."

He kept his eyes on her. If that's how she wanted to do this, he was game. He could play. And he could win. Like he had every other time she'd come at him with attitude.

"Are you trying to get a rise out of me?"

"No," she said, taking his drink from his hand and swallowing it in one gulp. "I'm trying to get you to admit the truth."

"And what truth is that?"

She ran her fingertip along the empty glass he held. "That you want me."

"You think so?"

She nodded. "I saw the way you looked at me." She leaned in. "The way you've *been* looking at me."

He took a deep breath. So she was challenging him. This was a game. Like it had been when they played Sardines. She'd call him out, and he'd shut her down.

"You think I want you, darlin'?"

The smile she unleashed was so devilishly sexy he was certain he'd imagined it.

She placed her hands on her hips and looked him dead in the eye. "I know you do."

Damn, confidence was a good look on her. Made him think for a moment she might be able to handle the hedonist he was deep down.

"Even if you were right, what would your brother say about that?"

"Ryder has nothing to do with this."

"There is no *this*."

She bit her bottom lip. It was more of an insecure gesture than the licking, but it still made his dick hard just watching her teeth nibble the plump flesh.

"S-so, you don't want me?"

Bass stood there, knowing he should say something. It was one thing to scare her off, but he couldn't outright lie to her. Did he want her? Hell yes. But he couldn't say that, either, so he stayed silent.

Something flickered over her face faster than the strobe lights. Her auburn brows furrowed with a look of pissed-off intent.

"Well, that's fine," she said. "But I'm going to tell you what I want."

And the brazen was back in Miss Diamond. He couldn't help but indulge. "Please enlighten me."

She lifted her chin. "I want to fuck."

If he'd been drinking, he would have choked. Before he could say anything, she went on.

"And not just anyone. I wanted to fuck you. But since you're obviously too busy hiding in a corner, I'll be on my way to find someone else who will give me what I want."

"You mean like cowboy Rob who's waiting to get you a martini and feed you lines about how pretty your smile is?"

On cue, she smiled, and it was more than pretty. It was

fucking mesmerizing.

"Yes." She turned. To leave him. To go to another man. Only this time, he knew what she was looking for. And that set his internal fire to nuclear.

"Penelope!" he yelled over the music, loud enough that her shoulders tensed in shock, but she spun back to face him. There was so much he wanted to do, to say, but he stuck with the truth, no matter how much it sucked. "It would never work."

She leaned so close that her lips skimmed his earlobe, and tremors raced down his spine.

"No one would have to know." There was a nervous tremble in her voice.

"That's the least of my worries, darlin'. You have no idea what I'm capable of. What I'd do to an innocent thing like you." He sneered the words, because a sick part of him wanted to do every damn thing to her. Everything her lush little body would allow him to do. And when she realized the kind of man he was, she'd run.

"You could show me?" she said. Again, there was a breathy note in her tone. He didn't go for vanilla girls, but that was the problem. Nothing about Penny struck him as vanilla. Inexperienced, sure. But there was a fire in her that brought out his dark, dominant side. And he wanted to give in to her request so damn bad.

"I'm tired of being innocent." She raised her chin and finished with, "It's *you* who has no idea what *I'm* capable of." Her green glare hit him hard, and she strutted that perfect ass away from him and toward the cowboy who, yep, held a martini and waited near the bar for her.

God damn it!

He went to take a drink of his whiskey, only to be hit with an empty glass and the lingering scent of strawberry lip gloss.

She was playing with fire. Fire that he'd had under control until he watched the cowboy cup her hip.

Nope. Not just nope, but hell-fucking-nope was another man touching her.

Whatever prized control he had was flying out the window. He set his glass down on a nearby table and stormed over to her. He didn't say anything, didn't acknowledge her shocked expression when he took the drink from her hand and gave it to Asshole Cowboy.

The guy was about to protest, but Bass didn't give a shit. He grabbed Penny's hand and tugged her toward the dance floor.

"I'll be right back," she called to the cowboy, and Bass just tugged harder, weaving through the mass of gyrating people.

"No you won't," he yelled over the thumping music, glancing back at her.

"Where are you taking me?" she said, but he ignored her.

He continued to maneuver through people until he got to the other end of the club. There was a small nook in the corner where shadows encased them, and he pulled her around, then pressed her back against the wall, wedging her into the corner.

He placed his hands on either side of her head, caging her in with his body. He looked down at her, so close their noses brushed.

"You think I sulk in corners?" he said. "You want to tease me on purpose? Flaunt yourself like a treat I can't have, then tell me you're capable of handling me?" He shook his head, and her bright green eyes sparkled with anticipation. "I'm set to show you what it is I do to a woman like you in dark corners."

Her lips parted, and she rose to kiss him, but he jerked back. "Oh no, darlin'. You don't run this show. I do."

He pressed his hips against hers and cupped her throat in his palm. There was only one way to end this. He'd give her a glimpse of the man he was, and it'd be enough to make her run away. He'd never hurt her. He'd never hurt any woman, but he was a rough man. And she was the epitome of softness.

With one hand still on her neck, he reached between their bodies and slid his fingers up her inner thigh until they disappeared beneath her skirt.

"What are you doing?" she breathed. Her gaze darted around the club, checking to see if anyone noticed them. But Bass didn't need to look to know the shadows concealed them.

"You don't know?" he said. This would be the moment she'd break. She'd see his darkness, and she'd shove him off and run away.

He reached the lace of her panties and stifled a groan. They were wet. His plan of getting her to leave him was shot to hell, because only one thing mattered in that moment.

"Who made you wet?" he growled.

She frowned. "What?"

He moved her panties aside and ran two fingers along her damp slit. "You're wet," he said again. "I want to know who caused this."

And the answer better be him. Because if she said that

other asshole's name, he was likely to go beat the hell out of the prick.

"You did." She kept her eyes on his but subtly shifted her hips, as if begging him to deepen the contact. "Every time I see you I get…"

She glanced away, and he would have none of it. With his palm still cupping her throat, he used his thumb to flick her jaw, making her face him once more.

"You get what?"

"Turned on." Her eyes were so penetrating, like she could see right to his damn soul. "The way you look at me, the way you talk to me…all of it makes me hot."

"What about the way *you* talk?" he said, sliding his fingers along her sweet spot until she gasped. "You said you wanted to fuck?"

He teased her entrance, pushing only the tip of his finger inside.

"I said I wanted to fuck *you*." Her eyes were squeezed shut, her hands flat against the wall behind her. He'd trapped her, and she was submitting. It was so perfect. Like her instinct was to give in to him. And his was to dominate…and cherish.

"Pretty mouth like that shouldn't say such nasty words." He bit her bottom lip. "Especially when you may get more than you bargained for."

"I want it, Bass. I want you." When he didn't move, her eyes snapped opened and seared him with another challenging glare. "Stop thinking of me like some fragile doll and—"

He thrust his finger deep and she gasped.

"Is this what you wanted?" He retreated but then returned with two fingers, plunging home again. Feeling her wet heat grip him after he'd spent so many nights imagining this moment was like a dream come to life. "You're so tight. You can barely handle two fingers." He kept them there, buried inside, and stirred deep until she was scratching at the wall behind her. "And yet you say you're not fragile."

"I'm not!" she moaned between clenched teeth.

"Well, I'm not gentle." He thrust again, and her sheath clenched around him with the release he was denying her.

Jesus she was responsive. She was already on the brink of coming, and he'd not even done half the things he wanted.

"I like control." He thrust again. "A challenge."

She nodded.

"Look at you, trembling against the wall with my hand up your skirt in public."

Her breasts were ready to spill over the top from her heavy panting, but her brassy attitude remained. "Looks like I'm not so innocent after all."

"Oh? Is this something you do? Maybe with that fucking cowboy? Would it be him right now instead of me?" He surged his fingers as far as he could and flicked them, rubbing the sensitive spot inside.

Her eyes widened with surprise. She wanted to come. He could see it. Felt it in how she tensed around him. But he denied her. For her game. For her tricks. For his own fucking hate of wanting her so much.

"No…only you. I only want you."

"Why?" he snapped.

"B-because I trust you." Her words were so raw and honest, they hit him like a boot to the gut.

She trusted him.

The exact thing he needed when it came to his sexual

lifestyle, and yet the last thing he wanted to hear from her. Because she was the one woman who should be running from him, the one woman he shouldn't want as badly as he did.

He withdrew his hand and stepped back. Her eyes were glossy as they searched his face. He had to get a grip. He had to get out of there. Had to get *her* out of there.

"I'm taking you back to Diamond," he said. "Now."

Chapter Two

After a quick good-bye, Penny was in the front seat of Sebastian's SUV as he sped down the highway, heading toward their sleepy home town. Thank God their friends were drunk enough not to notice the heat in her cheeks or the crackling energy between her and Sebastian.

He'd been calm, like nothing had happened only seconds ago. He'd told Colt he was taking her home and, being the responsible attorney, made sure everyone had a plan for their own safe way home. All of them were staying in a nearby hotel until tomorrow. Which left her in the front seat, alone with the painfully sexy attorney.

"Are you going to say something?" she asked.

He glanced at her. It had taken all the courage she'd had tonight to pursue him the way she had. But when she'd caught a glimpse of the man he kept hidden, seen all his intensity unleashed, she'd morphed into a woman who would give him anything—everything—he asked for.

"You didn't act like I expected."

She frowned. "You were touching me in public. How did you think I'd respond?"

He just stared at the dark road ahead. "Differently," was all he said.

He looked mad. Had she somehow upset him? No... she'd seen that look before. He wore it every time she got the better of him.

"You thought I'd push you away, didn't you?" she whispered.

His heavy breath was all the answer she needed. He had formed a plan to get rid of her, and instead, he'd only made himself all the more irresistible.

He might give in to her yet. She just had to push a little harder. Enough to access the man he kept on a tight chain. The man she'd gotten a taste of only minutes ago at the club.

"You're going to ignore me now? Not say a word?" she asked, crossing her arms, looking out the front window at the spring night. "You had plenty to say earlier. Like how tight and hot I was—"

"That mouth of yours is going to be a problem."

"Oh, you do speak! *The problem* is, you say things like that and don't follow through."

He took another deep breath, as if holding on to his control by a thread. Heat and strength radiated from him.

She'd spent enough time with him to know how he worked. He was in process mode. Trying to think of what step to take next. Maybe how to put her back in the friend zone. No way she'd let that happen. She'd come too far. Wanted him too much, and she was now convinced he wanted her back.

"While you're busy being mute over there, why don't I tell you what I think?" She turned in her seat, resting her left elbow on the headrest. "You obviously have certain preferences when it comes to sex."

He scoffed. "You have no idea, darlin'. You're trying to sign up for something you can't handle."

"And yet you're the one who walked away, not me." She smiled at him, and she was delighted to see a spark in his eyes. Time to ram the challenge home. "Maybe you're the one who can't handle it."

A low growl came from his chest, the intensity in him threatening to explode. Let it. She wanted to see if this intensity carried over to the bedroom. He kept warning her, but how bad could he be?

Whatever he thought, she was determined to make one thing clear: "I'm not weak," she said.

"I know."

"Then why can't we…"

"I don't do relationships. Much less with my best friend's little sister."

"Ah yes, the notorious two week rule."

He frowned. "How do you know about that?"

She studied her nails. "I've heard things. As you've pointed out, Ryder is my older brother, and you two have talked. Besides, it's obvious. No one has ever seen you with a woman longer than a few appearances here and there."

"Then you know that this rule is unwavering. Two weeks is it. But you're not a short-term kind of woman."

She was tired of being told who she was and wasn't. And she was tired of him dodging her. "But you had no problem shoving your hand up my skirt."

He clenched the steering wheel. "You say things that goad me on purpose."

"Good! Stop pretending to be something you're not, and stop thinking that I can't handle your truth. I can. Actually," she pointed at him, "why don't you tell me what it is you think I can't handle? Then I'll stop defending myself, and you can get over this idea that I'm some weakling."

"I wouldn't just fuck you. I'd fuck you hard, in any way I wanted, any time I wanted. I'd tie you up, make you beg, make you scream, and I'd take pleasure every time you did either." He voice was low and thick and made her skin sting with excitement. "I'd spank your ass, punish that mouth of yours by sinking my cock deep in your throat. And then, when you're exhausted, panting, aching from the pleasure and certain you can't take anymore…" His dark eyes snapped to hers. "I'd do it all over again."

Her mind raced, throwing mental pictures of all the wicked things he'd painted. It was overwhelming and exciting. What he was describing sounded more like the big leagues than the minors she was currently stuck in, but she was ready to be traded up.

Put me in coach, I'm ready to play.

"Now look who's speechless," he said with a sly grin, as if thinking he'd just won and scared her off.

"Sorry, I was just imagining all those things you'd described and thinking which one we'd do first."

That caught him off guard, his dark brows slicing down when he glanced away, obviously wondering if he'd heard her right.

Oh, you heard me, lawyer boy.

"I want to experience sex," she said.

"How much experience do you even have?"

Time to admit the truth. "Eli was the only man I was ever with."

"That idiot you dated a few years ago?"

"Yeah."

"That it?"

She nodded, hating that insecurity was creeping in, but this was why it was so important.

"You two were together a year?"

"Six months," she said. "But we only had sex once."

"Are you fucking with me?" His voice was harsh, but not angry.

"No, it's true. I wanted to wait, turns out he had someone on the side. The same someone he's engaged to now."

"I heard he was coming into town soon."

She nodded. Small town like theirs, word traveled fast. Everyone knew everyone, and Eli was no exception.

"So that's what this is about. You want to get Eli back?"

"God no!" she shot out. "Yes, his coming into town with the woman he cheated on me with is…weird. But it made me realize how stagnant I've been. I've been letting what happened with him affect my sex life."

Or lack thereof.

She needed to move on for herself, but she needed to be prepared to face Eli. And wanted to feel confident when that encounter happened. But more than that, she wanted to finally understand what it meant to be passionate. To give in to the instincts she'd suppressed for far too long. To feel on fire for someone—on fire for Sebastian.

"I've seen you on dates," he said.

"Yeah, with men that I have nothing in common with.

And Ryder's only made dating more difficult."

"He just wants to protect you."

"I know, but I don't need protecting. I need freedom. Need to enjoy my life."

Eli had been a big obstacle. When she got the news about him coming to town, she'd known she would have to face down a painful moment. She was feeling increasingly more alone and isolated, and it was slowly suffocating her. Even if Sebastian only did two weeks at a time, surely it was enough for her to learn and have a chance to really move on with some experience under her belt. To find a man that she could be passionate about long term.

"Ryder scares most men off. The few guys that do come around are boring. Not the kind of men I'm interested in." *Nothing like you.* "I can't keep living like that."

"He scares the bad ones off. You're a white picket fence kind of woman. Not a…" He waved his hand absently.

"Not a what?" She looked down at herself, that stupid insecurity doubling. "Not a sexy woman?"

He hit her with a hard look. "I didn't say that."

"You didn't have to. Everyone treats me like I'm some adorable doll."

"You're a good girl."

"But that's not all I am."

"I know. But you deserve *good* things. You're a relationship kind of woman. The marrying kind. And I'm not interested in either." He shook his head.

Yes, she was interested in those things. Her parents had a great marriage, and she'd always wanted the same for herself one day. But she also wanted to ditch the chastity belt and feel like a woman. And she needed Bass's help with that. She had to seal this deal before she lost him for good. This was her one chance to lay it all out there.

"What if I'm not looking for a relationship? I can be discrete."

He raised a brow. "You planned this, didn't you? This game of seduction."

"I had a mission—"

"And I was your target."

Penny was silent, and she couldn't tell if he was pissed, or really pissed. Sure, she'd gone into this with him as her target, but it was because she trusted him. Had her whole life. Because over the years, he'd demonstrated time and again that he cared about his friends. Including her. He wouldn't hurt her, but he could have a sharp bark...and maybe even a sharper bite.

"So let me get this straight," he said. "You set out to seduce me tonight, hoping we'd fuck around in secret?"

"Something like that," she mumbled.

She wanted experience, and she wanted *him*. Whatever he'd give her. So what if he usually dated out of town women for a short period of time? She was tired of living in a bubble.

She could do short term if it meant they'd finally stop dancing around what both of them wanted. She was determined to move on. To explore her sexuality and stop living like an empty shell of a woman.

"If you won't help, that's fine. But I'm done with celibacy. I'm done letting my heavy-handed brother dictate who's suitable dating material. And I'm for damn sure done watching life happen around me. I'm going to do this with or without you. But I want it to be with you."

His jaw clenched, and she hoped to God she hadn't just

overplayed her hand.

After an agonizingly long moment, he spoke. "Are you sure you know what you're asking? Sure you can handle what I'd offer? "

"You like control," she said, repeating his words from earlier and trying not to smile. She could hear the hunger in his voice. With any luck, he was moments from signing on for a sexy exploration with her. "I can handle that."

"Yes, but it's more than that. I like hard and rough, and when it comes to the woman I'm with, however short a time, she's mine."

"Yours? Like you own her?"

He glanced at her. "For the time we're together, she's mine. Totally and completely. I wouldn't call it ownership, more of a strict understanding. Until our time is up or she says no."

A tremor of anticipation raced through her. She liked the idea of him wanting her to that extreme. She also liked having him. It wasn't a bad thing in her mind. It made her feel valued. Protected, in a very different way than she was used to.

"Trust is key," he said. "You'd have to trust me to know your body. I'd have to trust you to be honest. Trust that you'd tell me no when you feel uncomfortable, and trust that you'd keep our time together a secret."

Yes, their "relationship" would be best kept between them. Because their tightknit group of friends would likely have their own reaction if they found out exactly what was going on. Ryder knew about Bass's short-term policy, and if he found out Penny was in the rotation, he'd freak. Likely so would the rest of their friends, thinking she needed to be protected. But she didn't want protection. She wanted domination.

"Yes, I understand," she said.

"I can give you lessons in sex, but the minute you say no, it ends. I respect that word implicitly."

"What if I never say no?"

"Then we work in a timeframe of two weeks."

"Why two weeks? I mean, I know you don't do long term, but how did you choose fourteen days as your timeframe?"

"Anything longer and emotions tend to cloud the situation." He said that so bluntly, like he'd experienced this problem before.

"Colt and Jenna are getting married in two weeks."

"Yes. So come that time, we're done. If you even last that long."

She swallowed hard. He was trying to make it sound scary, but all she heard was the adventure and excitement in this new arrangement. A short-term arrangement. Which left her wondering, "Then what?"

"Then we go back to being friends. No one is any the wiser."

She pursed her lips. "And Ryder?"

"I don't like the idea of lying to my best friend, but if you're set on fucking someone—" He took a deep breath, and those dark eyes pierced her. "I'd rather it be me."

His internal struggle was clear. She didn't want to put him in a situation to lie to Ryder, but she wasn't willing to give up this chance with the one man that made her feel more like a woman than a girl.

She looked at him for a long moment. He was so starkly beautiful. Dark hair and eyes, thick lips that set into a stern line. He was chiseled out of lean muscle, and his black tee fit tight around his chest and biceps. What *could* a man like him do to her?

She wanted to find out. Might die if she didn't.

"So we'd be together during the rehearsal dinner." It was the night before the wedding, and one Penny was looking forward to. She was hosting and catering it.

"We would not *be together*," he said. "Privately, yes. But publicly, no. Not at the rehearsal."

Looked like she would go stag to the rehearsal then. Which was fine. Because like he'd said, at least in private, they'd be together.

"Okay," she said. "So we're in agreement." She rested her hand on his knee.

"First lesson," he said, keeping his eyes on the road. "Take that hand and put it on your breast."

She opened her mouth to speak, but he shot her a hard stare, so she did as she was told. She took her hand from his knee and cupped her breast. He stole a glance. Just that quick look made her nipples harden and her skin buzz with need. This was out of her element. She'd never done such a thing in front of someone before.

When her hand slowed and uncertainty crept in, he said, "Both hands, rub your breasts. Close your eyes and imagine it's me."

She glanced down at the one hand she already had on herself.

"This is part of the game, darlin'. If you don't want to play, you know the word to say."

She took a deep breath to regain her focus. She had to keep her eye on the prize. Sebastian's approval.

She nodded and reached with both hands now to caress her breasts. Still unsure, she kept her touch soft.

"Remember, I told you to think of me." He lifted his chin at her ministrations. "Do you think that's how I'd touch you?"

"No," she whispered. He would be intense. He'd consume her. Just thinking of his big strong hands—how he'd grip her, how he'd take her—made her own touch roughen.

Would he bite? The idea shot a jolt of pleasure through her. She pinched her nipples, imagining it was his teeth—

"Now spread your legs wide."

She paused to process his request, but he didn't allow her to overthink it.

"Your legs. Spread. Them."

She did. And eyes close, she waited for his instruction. Part of her wanted to look at him. The other part was happy her eyes were closed. It allowed her to be more bold. Focus on his voice. His presence.

The anticipation built, but he stayed quiet. Was he looking at her? Was he bored already? The time that passed could have been seconds or minutes, but it felt like forever.

She wanted him so much, her body begging for the orgasm he'd denied her earlier, and now her nerves and lack of experience swirled, her insecurity rising, and just when she was about to open her eyes and make sure he was still in the car, he broke the silence.

"Reach between those pretty thighs and rub your clit."

Relief raced through her. She lifted one hand, wondering if she could really do this but eager to prove she could—

"Slowly," he said. "Sometimes waiting is the hardest part. But you're in my world now."

That's when it hit her. All the things he'd spoken of earlier, what he could do to her body, the one thing he hadn't promised was the one thing she feared the most: distance.

He could keep her on edge. Not touch her. Not speak to her. And that was where the torture came in. He was gauging how much she really could let go and trust him.

"I told you to do something. Don't make me repeat myself."

She swallowed hard and did as told. The edge in his voice made her want to drink down every rough syllable. How could his voice—his commands—alone make her feel this aching need?

Pushing her panties aside, she used the moisture Bass had coaxed from her earlier to slide her fingers along the sensitive bundle of nerves. She'd never touched herself in front of someone before. But he was different. This was what she wanted to learn, and he was providing.

She'd only rubbed three slow circles and already was on the brink of coming.

"Good girl," he rasped. His approval sent shivers up her body. If only it was his hands on her. "Now sink your fingers inside. Just like I did earlier."

"Yes," she said and instantly obeyed. Her skin was hot, her lungs stretching from lack of air. She was close...but the tremors slowly fizzled as she slid her fingers inside and realized it wasn't the same as what Sebastian made her feel.

"Don't you want to come, darlin'?" he asked.

"Yes, but I..." She shifted her hips, still keeping her eyes closed she frowned. "I can't reach."

She was at the edge of bliss, but she couldn't get there. Not without him.

She let out a frustrated huff. "It's not the same without

you." Her words came out soft and almost pained. "I need you…"

The car went from a smooth glide to bumpy in seconds. She opened her eyes to find he'd pulled onto a desolate gravel road off the highway and parked. She couldn't say a word before he got out of the car, stalked around the front, and threw her door open.

"Did I do something wrong?" she asked.

Bass unclasped her seatbelt, grabbed her ankle, and spun her so that her legs dangled outside the car. With the gravel crunching beneath his boots, he stepped between her thighs.

"No, you didn't do anything wrong." He cupped her nape with one hand and plunged the other between her legs. "I want you to come, and I want to feel it."

Just like at the club, he thrust two fingers deep inside of her and rubbed that spot she couldn't reach.

"Oh God, yes." She gripped his shoulders.

"Is that what you need?" His voice sounded just as desperate and raspy as hers had. He rubbed faster, his fingers working magic deep inside of her. "Right there?"

"Yes, yes right there."

"Then come for me."

Penny was helpless against him. She obeyed, like she had from the moment he'd started this lesson. With his name on her lips, she cried out as her body shuttered her over the edge in a hot, heady kick of ecstasy.

"There's my good girl," he said, continuing his assault on her sensitive flesh. "Come on, you can do better. Give it up. All of it."

His thumb brushed over her clit while his other fingers

remained deep, taking her orgasm to a whole new level.

"Sebastian!" She screamed his name and dug her nails into his back. All she could do was hold on as her body tensed and released, her climax so hard that she felt dizzy from the pleasure.

"There you go," he whispered in her ear as his ministrations became slower and softer, bringing her down from the intense pleasure.

His grip on her nape tightened, and she opened her eyes. She might be sitting in her seat, but Bass was supporting her limp body and staring down at her.

"Next time, you'll do that around my tongue."

Penny swallowed hard and nodded. It sounded like a half promise, half threat. And she was anxious for either.

Chapter Three

I need you…

Those three words Penny had said last night hadn't left his thoughts since.

Sebastian had been out to teach her a lesson. She might be wholesome, but she was a wiry woman with a temper that tested his patience. So he had to see if she could allow him to control the situation. Establish that her pleasure was in his hands, even when he put it—literally—in her own. Then in one, sweet, breathy plea, he'd thrown the playbook out and become consumed with his own need.

Her.

"Looks like you need a beer," Ryder said, walking up to Sebastian.

Standing outside Penny's BBQ, the place they met every Sunday for lunch and to shoot the shit, they shook hands and then headed inside. Thank God Rocco ran the restaurant on Sundays, giving Penny her weekends off.

Facing down one Diamond would be difficult enough, much less two.

"Yeah, maybe a couple beers," Bass said. Because Penny had said something else. She'd asked, *What if I never say no?*

Bass had to hold back a scoff, because eventually, she would. She'd walk away. Whether that was today or two weeks from now, someone always did.

They made their way to the booth near the pool table. The wood floor creaked as they walked, and the smell of barbecue sauce and the sound of the old jukebox put him instantly at ease. This was the closest thing to home Bass knew. Sure, he had a house, some land, and his law practice on Main Street. But a home? When he thought of such a thing, the name "Diamond" always came up.

Sebastian's dad had been a mean son of a bitch. After his mom had left, his dad had shown no problem taking out his anger on Bass, especially when he'd been drinking.

He hadn't always been like that. Sebastian remembered how his father had once smiled. Before his mother left. Yes, Walt Strafford was an ass, but it was because Gretta Strafford had stolen his heart. His happiness. His faith in women. Something he'd ranted about over the course of Sebastian's life.

Bass had needed somewhere to escape, and thank God he'd found the BBQ. From grade school to high school, Mrs. Diamond always had a place for him and made him feel welcome. When she'd passed away last year and Penny took over, he'd found himself still coming for solace, only the Diamond woman that greeted him made his chest ache in a way he didn't understand.

And now I'm involved with that Diamond woman.

There was a guilt that went with that. Another emotion

he didn't do well. But when he made up his mind, he stuck to it. Penny wasn't a bluffer. She had a mission, and he believed her when she said she'd go on this sexual exploration with or without him.

No fucking way was it going to be without him.

Of course, that meant lying to his best friend. But in some sick way, he thought—hoped—that her being with him was better than whoever else she could find out there. He'd never take advantage of her innocence the way some men would. Which made him an even sicker son of a bitch, because part of him liked that she was innocent. That she was fresh and naïve, and he would be the one to tap into her wild side. To teach her.

But he figured he wouldn't get the chance to dirty her up too bad. He had a solid plan. She'd call their secret fling off the moment he slapped her ass or pulled out the cuffs. Of that he was certain.

"How was the meeting?" he asked, sliding into the booth across from Ryder.

Ryder adjusted his worn Stetson and put his forearms on the table. "It was all right. They liked my bid, liked my business, but I guess it's between Diamond Construction and another company. They'll let me know next week. If we can land this, we'd be set for the year."

Bass nodded. Ryder had built and owned his own construction and land development company. Several years back, Huck had bought a stake in the business and become a co-owner. But he left the negotiations to Ryder, preferring to swing hammers over talking business. Their group was close and always supported each other. They were the one thing he held sacred.

Which was why he knew he was fucking around with fire when it came to Penny. He was putting the few things he cared about in jeopardy. His trust with Ryder. The dynamic of their entire group of friends. His strictly platonic—up until recently—friendship with Penny.

Maybe he'd been too hasty. He'd dropped her off last night, alone, because he had to think. Hardest thing he'd ever done was decline an invitation inside her home. But now, in the light of day, staring at Ryder, he was glad he hadn't crossed all the lines yet.

Maybe he should call her up, talk to her and try to talk her out of this mission of sex or whatever the hell kick she was on. End this before he actually did all the things he'd said he would do.

Yes, *that* was smart.

"Afternoon, boys," a musical voice rang out. He looked up to find the most beautiful woman staring down at him, holding two long neck beers.

"Hey sis," Ryder said.

"Why are *you* here?" Sebastian asked before he could catch himself.

Both Ryder and Penny looked at him with surprise. Jesus, where were his manners, let alone charm? He might not be like Huck and Colt with the country boy swagger, but he held his own. Especially with the ladies.

"Forgive me, darlin'," he said. "I just thought today was your day off."

"Yeah," Ryder said. "Especially if you had a late night last night, you should be resting. Was the party fun?"

Penny shot a glance at him and placed the beers on the table. Leaning over just enough to give a peek of that incredible cleavage concealed by a tight black tank top. He stifled a groan. What had he been thinking again? Oh, right, calling it off with Penny.

The smart thing, he reminded himself.

He looked her over. All that red hair was piled on top of her head, little strands hanging down to frame her face. He examined all the alabaster skin from her back to her chest, then down to her legs, which were barely concealed in a pair of cutoffs and a short apron. Every curve was on display, every inch of perfection.

Shit. Calling it off was going to be a problem when all he could think of was how the crook between her neck and shoulder tasted. Did the shimmer on her lips taste like strawberries?

He'd bet his salary they did.

"It was okay," she shrugged, placing one hand on the table and the other on her hip. "And I wasn't out that late. Bass here gave me a ride home."

Ryder shot a look at him. "I thought everyone was going to stay the night in the city."

"Yeah, I thought the same thing," she said, smiling at Sebastian. "*Staying the night* would have been fun."

That time he didn't miss the sugary sweet challenge in her voice. Looked like she was pissed he had left her. He wasn't any happier about it either, but he'd had to gather himself.

Now, staring down the gorgeous woman with the afternoon sun bleeding through the windows and haloing her like a damn angel, he had a hard time not kicking his own ass for passing up an entire night with her.

Soon.

Fuck calling it off. He had to surround himself by all that sweet skin. Bury himself so deep into that sexy body neither of them could breathe. And what better way to prepare her for what was to come than to meet her challenge right now?

"Staying the night wasn't a good idea," he said, looking her straight in the eye. "And what do you mean last night was *okay*? You looked to be enjoying yourself to me."

She licked her lips, and damn if he didn't love this. This silent waging of wills. A secret competition.

Ryder was sitting right there. This whole conversation was a bad idea, but he couldn't help it. Penny had laid it out there, challenged him, and he'd accepted.

She'd said she could be discrete? Well, he wove words and passively argued for a living. Game on.

"Maybe I was faking my enjoyment," she said, and Bass laughed. Honest to God laughed, which she clearly didn't appreciate. She straightened and nailed him with glare.

"What's so funny?" Ryder asked.

"Your sister is," he said. His face actually hurt from how wide he was smiling. "She couldn't fake a thing if she tried." He tilted his chin at her. "Look at those big honest eyes of hers." Not to mention, he felt her come apart.

Faked it, my ass.

She was just trying to goad him, but he knew better. He'd watched her fall over the edge and milk his fingers. The damn memory kept him up half the night with a hard-on that wouldn't go away.

Ryder chuckled, and Penny's cheeks heated. Her temper was rising. She might look sweet, but the petite woman had a flare in her that was sexy as hell. She'd pushed his buttons last night, and now it looked like Miss Diamond was getting a taste of her own medicine.

"He's right, sis. You wear your emotions like face paint. But why didn't you stay with the girls in the city?"

"Because," Bass said, facing his friend. "She had some admirers at the club. I thought it best to get her out of there."

Ryder nodded. "Good. I'm glad you were there. There's a lot of assholes in the city."

"I'm not some child that needs to be whisked away every time a guy hits on me," she snapped, that temper dialed to ten.

"Who was hitting on you?"

"Some asshole cowboy," Bass said.

"Will you stop talking about me like I'm not right here?" she said to Sebastian. "You're as bad as my brother."

He simply smiled and took a drink of his beer. "Ah, darlin', that's where you're wrong." He leaned her direction and snared her gaze. "I'm much, *much* worse."

• • •

Penny was going to scream. This kind of secret flirting was making her hot and pissed off all at the same time. She was ready to pull Bass up by the hair and kiss the hell out of him, or maybe just pull his hair.

He made her feel crazed, needy, brassy, and strong. When he dropped her off at the restaurant last night, she went to the backdoor to make the lonely trek up the stairs to her apartment above. An apartment she'd invited him into but he'd declined.

Today was supposed to be her day off, but she had to get her mind off last night, and work was the best distraction. That was why she'd come in. *Not* to see Bass…

She looked at his thick, dark hair, his strong chiseled jaw that held just a hint of five o' clock shadow even though it was only noon. The weekends were the best because he was casual, usually in jeans and T-shirts. Not that he didn't rock a suit, but it was maddening how effortlessly sexy the thin, white cotton crew neck clinging to his chest and abs made him as he sat there.

Yeah, she definitely had *not* worked on her day off just to gape at him...

She opened her mouth to say something, to beat him at his own game and keep this secret conversation going, but Huck threw open the front door and stomped in.

"Whoa, you look like shit," Ryder said as Huck plopped down beside him, forcing him to scoot over in the booth.

"Are those the same clothes you had on last night?" Sebastian asked.

"Yes." The normally laidback playboy rested his head between his hands and exhaled deeply.

"That good, huh? Hook up with a city girl?" Ryder asked. To which Huck answered with an annoyed growl. "Ah crap, tell me she didn't slash your truck tires like the last girl?"

"No," Huck said.

"Then what's wrong?" Penny asked, rubbing his shoulder.

Bass's eyes snapped to her movements, and a dark look came over his face. As if the attorney didn't like that she was touching Huck. They were just friends, he knew that. But still, it made her kind of giddy that he was in tune with every move she made.

"Don't want to talk about it." Huck's voice was barely a mumble.

"Men and their pride." She shook her head.

Huck had his own reasons he didn't get too serious with women. From what she understood, it was different than Sebastian's reasons. But still, most men in her world, friends or not, didn't like the commitment thing. That was up until Colt had fallen head over boots for Jenna.

"It's not a pride thing. Shitty stuff happens sometimes, and I don't want to get into it."

"All right, buddy." Ryder slapped his shoulder. "Sis, I think our boy needs a beer."

"I'll bring you all another round and some burgers too." She didn't spare Sebastian a glance as she turned and walked away. She didn't make it past table eleven when she heard someone call out her name.

"Hi, Penny," an unfortunately familiar voice said. It was Finn, taking a seat and pulling a laminated menu from its holder at the center of the table. "How are you?"

His smile was genuine, and he looked nice in white polo shirt and khaki pants. His hair was perfectly parted and combed, and his freshly shaved face, heck, everything about him, looked and smelled like generic shampoo. He was cute enough. Not crazy sexy in a dark way like some—rather one—man she knew. One dinner with him had let her know he was safe—too safe for her—but that had also put him in Ryder's "approval" category for her.

"I'm good," she said. "How about yourself?"

He nodded and threaded his fingers. "Good. I was hoping I'd see you." A small blush laced his face. "I was also going to ask when your days off were?"

Oh crap. She gave her kindest expression while she searched for words. Her gaze darted to the table Bass sat at. She almost stumbled as she found his dark eyes already locked on her. Ryder was also looking at her, and if only he knew better, but he was giving her a not so discrete thumbs up. Thank God Finn couldn't see. But Bass could.

"I um, my days off are kind of undetermined right now. Since I'm hosting the rehearsal dinner, I've been extra busy, and my schedule has been a little off."

"Oh, okay. That makes total sense. That's real great of you helping with the dinner. Especially with cooking like yours."

"That's sweet of you," she said. Finn was a nice guy. The right kind of guy. Rather, the kind that was supposed to be right for her. Only nothing about him felt right. He had similar goals for life as her. Wanted to settle down and start a family. But there was no fire with him. She chanced a look at Sebastian again. He sat motionless, listening to whatever Huck was saying, now not sparing her a glance.

"What can I bring you to eat?" she asked, hoping to get out of the conversation and away for some space and air.

He glanced at the menu. "I'll have the cobb salad and an iced tea, please."

She smiled and nodded, jotting down his order. Right next to the order for burgers and beers for Bass's table.

There was a difference between a burger and a cobb salad. For some reason, in that moment, it seemed like a *big* difference.

"I'll get that going for you," she said and took off. She wove around the bar and back to the kitchen, she put an order in for the cook to start on some burgers.

The bottled beer was getting a little low behind the counter, so she hustled through the kitchen and around back to the storage area to grab a few more cases. She'd lifted a box when the door closed behind her.

She spun to find Sebastian leaning back against the door, thumbs hooked in his leather belt, staring her down.

"What are you doing?" she breathed, tamping down the surprise.

Though his stance was casual, his eyes were intense. Every muscle in his strong body was honed, as if ready to attack.

She felt a charge humming through her body. From her breasts to her thighs and everything in between.

"I'm hungry." His voice was deep, quick, and cut through the air, sending chills over her back.

"I put in for your burgers. They'll be done soon."

"No." He pushed himself off the door and took one, two, three easy strides towards her. "I want something specific."

He took the case of beer out of her hands and set it on the floor.

"You seem a bit wily today, darlin'." His hands slowly wrapped around her, and in a millisecond, he untied her apron and dropped it to the floor.

"I um…" She stared at his mouth, breathing in his crisp scent of pine and all things masculine. Between him messing with her inner temperature and running into Finn while her brother all but threw a party, she was a frazzled mess of nerves. But where had her temper gone? Oh yeah, it had deflated when she looked at Sebastian's hot gaze and perfect lips.

"I'm annoyed," she finally managed.

"Oh?" His fingers trailed along her waist until landing on the button of her shorts. "Want to tell me why?"

She closed her eyes, struggling to find words as those fingers she'd become well acquainted with popped the button of her shorts open and pushed them down her legs until they were next to the apron on the ground.

"You," she whispered. "You annoy me."

"Hmmm…" He skimmed his thumb along her panties, then hooked it in the lacy band and tugged them off. "I'd prefer a different adjective when describing how I make you feel. Let's see what I can do to make you happy with me."

His cool palm gripped behind her knee, raising her leg and resting one foot on the case of beer. Her hands instantly flew out, clutching his chest to keep her balance. She may not have bottoms on, but she was still wearing her boots.

"I-I thought you liked control."

He frowned. "I do." He covered her hands with his and slid them up his hard chest until they reached his face. He kissed her palm. "But I also told you I want what I want, when I want. Don't mistake my like of control to be a selfish endeavor."

He slowly sank to his knees, the action causing her hands to go from his face to the top of his head as he knelt before her.

Pressing his nose against her inner thigh, he took a deep breath. "Fuck I've been thinking about this for a long time."

Her whole body shook with anticipation as his lips brushed her skin. "Then why didn't you stay with me last night?"

He glanced up at her. "Because sometimes anticipation is the best part."

"And you control the anticipation," she said, the truth hitting her. It wasn't all black and white with him. Last night he was fierce, today he was flirty, but the end was the same.

He's always in control.

This was definitely going to be more of a learning experience than she realized. Not just about sex, but about him. A snip of uncertainty crept in. Could she really keep up with him? She hoped so. Wanted to so badly, but that word from her past rang in her mind: vanilla. She didn't want to be boring, didn't want to be lacking. Not with him. Not ever again.

"Tell me," he said, delivering kisses on her thigh as he continued to get closer to the spot that was dampening by the second. "Have you ever been eaten?"

She shook her head. "No."

A mixture of a growl and a sigh came from low in his throat.

"I'm the first." It wasn't a question, rather a statement. But hearing it out loud made her blood pick up rhythm, and if she wasn't mistaken, Sebastian's too.

"Yes."

"Then I should warn you…" He delivered one long lick between her folds, and her grip on his hair tightened. "I'm not going to eat you, I'm going to *devour* you."

He sank his tongue deep, and she gasped, an instant tremor shooting through her body like a comet on the horizon.

With one arm threaded around her thigh, the other reached up and tugged down her tank top and bra, exposing one breast. He pinched her nipple, and she moaned loudly.

"Shhh, don't want to get caught now do you? I'd have to stop."

She folded her lips together in agreement. "Please don't stop."

With a wicked smile, he went back between her legs, only this time, he snaked that incredible tongue over her clit.

"Oh God," she whispered between clenched teeth.

He flicked the sensitive spot over and over, then delved deep inside again to taste what he'd wrought from her.

"You're like strawberries," he muttered, then started the whole torturous routine over again.

The man wasn't a liar. He was in fact devouring her. Lapping and sucking. Coaxing every ounce of pleasure and building it to a peak that she couldn't fight. She watched his strong jaw move and his brows draw tight, like he was tasting the finest dessert and concentrating on experiencing every morsel.

Just when she thought he'd gently take her over the edge and give her a nice, slow climax, he closed his teeth over her clit and sucked hard.

"Oh, fuck!" she screamed when the sharp sting turned into heady lust and raced through her. "Bass," she whispered, but it came out more of a strangled breath. "I'm going to come."

Not just come, she was going to burst into a thousand pieces. The nip of pain, mixed with the hot suction of his mouth made her body jolt with such intensity, she barely kept herself upright.

The case of beer her foot rested on shook. As her body trembled, the sound of glass bottles gently dinging against each other echoed in the small storage room.

Cupping her whole breast, he massaged and squeezed with the right amount of pressure to send her flying even further over the edge. Zings of pleasure shot through her as he buried his tongue deep one final time. His fingers dug into her thigh as he clutched her closer to him, drawing out the bliss and drinking her down as she moaned his name.

It didn't end. Nothing had ever felt so good. So sexy and wicked. And he kept going. Plunging deep, like he couldn't get enough. With her head thrown back and nails digging into his scalp, she had no choice but to let the explosive orgasm keep coming. Over and over. And Bass was right there to catch her.

With a few lingering licks, he rose to his feet and faced her. She was breathless and trembling.

"That was lesson number two," he said with a husky pride that made her melt another degree. "Challenging me in public only brings out my competitive side."

"I didn't—"

"You want to claim that you just *faked* that too?"

She snapped her mouth shut. Oh, that. Yeah, she'd said that to piss him off. Instead, he'd used it as a reason to remind her that her pants were on fire from the fib.

He grinned and ran his thumb along his lower lip, then sucked it.

"Mmmm. Tastes like sweet, sweet victory." With that, he turned, opened the storage door, and left, closing the door behind him.

She stood there, bare from the waist down, one breast out and her mouth hanging open in a daze.

Another point for the lawyer. It was the second time he'd gotten the better of her body, then walked away. It wasn't lost on her that he'd not only *not* had sex with her, but he also hadn't kissed her. Well, on the mouth at least.

This was a game. And her lessons were only making her more and more greedy for what he held back. He could have his control, but she needed to tap into her strength.

Through the door, she heard the faint ding of the bell, followed by the cook's rumbling voice.

"Order up!"

Chapter Four

The smell of roses and carnations engulfed the room as Penny wound through the chilled little hut, looking at centerpiece options with Jenna.

"Thank you so much for doing this with me," Jenna said.

The wedding flowers had been picked out a while ago, but Penny thought brightening up the tables with some decor would be nice. The entire event was her wedding present to Colt and Jenna. While the menu and preparations were a bit stressful, she loved the event.

Weddings were fun. And this was the closest she had ever come to one. Marriage and a family were things she wanted eventually. Actually, if she were honest, she'd hoped eventually would be sooner than later. She knew now she had some personal growth to finish first, and she'd thought Sebastian would be the thing that put her on the fast track.

But he hadn't spoken to her since yesterday's storage room scandal. A climatic event that had her blood still racing and her body on fire.

She'd known the man for the majority of her life, yet after the past couple of days, the term "knowing him" was rapidly evolving. There'd been lust in his eyes, and even though she knew better than to hope for more, she found herself wondering "what if?"

But she couldn't tackle that idea. She had another question pressing into her thoughts since the other day: How?

How could he make her feel the way she did—sexy and sinful—but also make her feel crazed, annoyed with just a hint of comfort? Like the second she was in his grasp, his hands would never let her stray too far. And how would things be between them after the two weeks? She didn't even know how tomorrow would be.

She shook her head, the questions frustrating and irritating because she didn't have an answer to any of them. All she could do was wait…and hope for another stolen moment with the powerful attorney. Maybe then she'd have a better idea of how to handle these hot flashes.

"You okay?" Jenna asked, snapping Penny back to the present.

"Yeah, sorry I was spacing out." She smiled and looked at her friend, who was beaming with joy. "I'm excited to be here with you."

"Me too. Glad you were able to get off work."

"Rocco covered for me today since I worked yesterday," Penny said, adjusting her purse. Jenna also had today off, so it worked out well that they could go together.

"I feel like I haven't seen you as much," Jenna said.

"It's been busy. You're planning a wedding, which understandably takes up a lot of time. But we need to hang out every chance we can before you're barefoot and pregnant."

Jenna smiled. "We'll still hang out. Even when I'm Mrs. McCade."

"I know." But she also knew things were changing.

Jenna was amazing and deserved everything wonderful in the world. And her world was Colt. It was more than apparent that Colt's universe was Jenna.

The idea of settling down, having a couple kids and an adoring husband, had always appealed to Penny, but that dream was a far cry from realistic these days. She was still trying to figure out sex. But the rest? The future full of laughter and kids and the PTA...that dream would have to wait, no matter how badly she ached for it.

Someday...

Yeah, maybe. If she was lucky. The way things were going, she'd forever be the "wholesome" baby sister of Ryder Diamond who no one took seriously. She'd be stuck swooning over a dark eyed attorney from afar.

No, she'd be confident, she reminded herself. Once their two weeks were up, she'd know what she wanted in a man... and what she wanted in the bedroom. That was the agreement. He would teach her, their time would eventually end, and then she'd move on, ready to take control of her dating life.

"You left so quickly the other night at the club that you never told me how things went. I'm assuming that since Bass took you home you didn't have a chance to...you know..." Jenna wiggled her eyebrows.

This was the part Penny hated. Fibbing. Jenna was one of her best friends, and she couldn't say what had really happened that night, or yesterday in her storage cellar for that matter. But she could stick to the truth the best she could.

"I didn't have sex."

"So the operation still needs to be carried out," Jenna mumbled, and Penny saw her mind working.

"You're not plotting something are you?"

Jenna gently touched one of the white calla lily center pieces and shrugged. "Plot? Never. I just have some ideas."

Penny sighed. "Please, no more blind dates. Besides, I don't want to deal with Ryder being all pissy and giving me the third degree when he finds out."

"You say that like I already have someone in mind."

Penny raised a brow. Jenna just waved the conversation and off switched subjects. Crap, Jenna was totally going to set her up.

Before she could protest further, Penny's phone buzzed, and she fished it out of her purse.

It was a text from Sebastian. She resisted the urge to jump up and down and giggle like a girl just asked to winter formal.

Bass: *I have a craving for strawberries…*

Her cheeks instantly heated. She wrote back.

Penny: *Is that so?*

A few seconds went by, and she stared at her phone. Jenna said something about a different vase of flowers, and Penny absently nodded.

Bass: *Yes. I find it a craving I have yet to satisfy since the other day. Are you ready for your next lesson? It will require your undivided attention.*

Penny: *I'm a pretty studious woman. Should I have*

something to take notes with?

Bass: *That mouth of yours is going to get you into trouble.*

Penny: *I'm just trying to figure out how much time to block out of my day. Since our last encounters have been rather quick. Thought you'd have more stamina, that's all.*

Bass: *The next time you see me, I'll show you stamina.*

Penny smiled and put her phone back in her purse. She looked up to find Jenna, arms crossed and staring at her.

"What?"

"You haven't heard a word I said, huh?"

"I said the flowers were nice." Though, no, she hadn't heard a thing, but she assumed the flowers were a smart jumping off point.

"The only time I get that blushy while texting is when Colt is sexting me something naughty."

That made her blush harder, but this time with nervousness to cover her ass.

"Oh, that was just Rocco, telling me something funny that happened at the BBQ today."

Jenna eyed her for a long moment, as if trying to believe her.

"I like these," Penny said, pointing to a square vase of dahlias, but Jenna wasn't derailed.

"So, since last weekend was a bust, you still need to get some," Jenna said. "This weekend will be a perfect time to try out your bad girl alter ego again."

Well, at least they weren't talking about her sexting anymore.

"This weekend is the party at the lake."

Jenna nodded. Every year around Memorial Day weekend, the majority of Diamond's town folk headed out to the lake for barbequing, swimming, and relaxing. It was a big event on the outskirts of Diamond property. But there was only one person Penny was interested in seeing.

"Do you know who all's going?"

Jenna frowned. "Most of the town."

Penny rolled her eyes. "I mean of our friends. Ryder's been traveling more, and I'm not sure if he'll be there, but do you know about Huck, Lily, and Bass?"

Real smooth.

"I don't know. I think they'll all be there. I know Alex is super excited."

Alex was Lily's six-year-old son and about the cutest thing on the planet.

Jenna came to a small bouquet of lilies, pink roses, and daisies. "What do you think of this? We can put them in mason jars to make it look all down-homey."

"You're getting married at a nice hotel in the city. But you want mason jars?"

"It fits the rehearsal dinner at the BBQ. Keeps things simple."

"If that's what you want."

Jenna nodded. "I know there's extra stress on you with the rehearsal dinner coming up and you worrying about Eli. I can't thank you enough for hosting and cooking."

"I'm happy to help, Jenna," Penny said, grabbing the

bouquet and heading toward the register.

"I know the other night didn't go as you planned, but are you doing okay?"

It definitely hadn't gone as planned, but she wasn't too bummed out. How could she be with that last text Bass had sent?

"Yeah, I'm good. I'm just going to focus on the dinner coming up and postpone Operation: Orgasm." By postpone, she meant carry it out in secret with Sebastian, but again, those were things she couldn't say out loud.

"Are you worried about running into Eli?"

"Kind of. Not as much as I was." Mostly because in the forty-eight hours she'd been with Sebastian, she was already feeling stronger. Happier.

Jenna looked at her for a moment.

"What?" Penny finally asked under the scrutiny.

"You seem…different."

She shrugged and tried to keep the guilt off her face. "I'm just excited for the future. There's good stuff coming."

Of that, she was certain. Until she saw the devious look on Jenna's face. She knew her friend too well, and Penny had an idea she was going to be on the losing end of some secret scheme here real quick.

"Yes," Jenna said happily. "Lots of good stuff is bound to happen in the future."

Jenna had no idea how right she was. Penny's future, at least for the next several days, involved finding out how good Sebastian the sex god could be.

Chapter Five

Penny walked through her front door and set her purse down. Flower shopping with Jenna had been fun, but with night falling, she was ready for a hot shower.

Out of nowhere, she was grabbed from behind. One palm covered her mouth while the other wrapped around her waist. "You should really start locking your door," a husky voice said.

She'd recognize that voice anywhere.

Sebastian.

"All you have to do is tell me no," he said. His grip tightened, pressing her ass into his front. She could feel him hard against her. "Tell me no. Tell me to unhand you and leave, and I will. Otherwise—" he thrust "—you're mine. However I want you. And it won't be gentle."

Between him walking away after the club and yesterday from the storage closet, she wasn't about to let him go anywhere. Besides, her body was already on fire to find out how he'd back up all those sinful promises.

He slowly removed his hand from her mouth, allowing her to speak.

Did he think he'd scared her into saying no? Now that he was finally in her house and promising sex?

Though her nerves were a bit frazzled from the surprise of him being there, she gathered her composure and looked over her shoulder to meet his eyes. "Adding breaking and entering to your list of skills, counselor?"

He frowned. Looked like he *had* been thinking she'd say no.

Not today, buddy. Time to pay up or shut up. If there was one thing she knew how to do, it was provoke him. If she wanted the full experience, she'd have to push.

"I thought you were hardcore?" she said, then turned back to study her nails. "I'll give you credit, you surprised me, but now you just stop? It looks like you're really good at delivering empty promises."

What could only be described as a growl came from him, and before she knew it, he clung to her waist like a vice and moved her into the kitchen.

"I've been warning you about that mouth." He bent her over the kitchen table. "It's going to get you into trouble." He hiked up her skirt around her waist, baring her ass. A loud snap sounded and a sting of pain shot through her as his open palm came down on her ass.

She cried out. He reached forward and grabbed her chin, making her look back at him.

"That was a soft one, darlin'. You sure you still want to play this game?"

She nodded. The pain held a mix of pleasure, and it was

humming through her like sparklers ignited against her skin.

"Brave girl," he said, releasing her chin. All she could do was stand there, bent over her kitchen table, ass in the air, while he stood behind her.

She waited. Then felt the barest touch of his finger tip trace along the spot he'd just smacked.

"Your skin is so perfect. Ivory. I can see my hand-print…" He traced up, down, up, as if outlining the fingers of the mark. "It's pink and hot. But does it make you hot?" He grabbed her hair in his fist. "Or does it make you scared?"

"Not scared," she said. "I want more."

He released her and palmed her ass. Then another smack came, then another. She clenched her teeth. Hard and rough, just like he'd promised, and it made her crazed. She'd never known things like this could feel good, but being bent, liter-ally, to his will was beyond thrilling, it was overwhelming.

Her ass was on fire, her skin buzzing. She wiggled a little, realizing that yes, she was wet. Just the spanking made her body ready and hot, and it was all for him. Something he must have realized, because she felt his mouth kiss along the marks he'd left.

"You constantly challenge me, say things to get me worked up." He bit her cheek, then sucked, causing her to moan. "You wanted sex? Passion? To be taught and have experiences?"

A loud rip ran through the air as he tore her panties clean off. She tried to keep quiet, because she wanted him to keep going.

He grabbed her hands and brought them behind her back. Her breasts and the side of her face pressed into the table as he fastened the tattered fabric of her panties around her wrists, binding them behind her.

She wanted to ask what he was doing. Ask for him to finally take her. But she was scared that if she spoke, he'd stop. So she arched her back and heard the unclasping of a belt and clothes hit the floor. His clothes.

He was getting naked? She tried to look behind her, but he smacked her ass again.

"You stay where I put you."

"I just want to see you." She wiggled her wrists. "Touch you."

"This is my time. I told you I like control. I'm going to fuck you. I'll let you know when you can touch me."

She bit her lip. Something about his low, raspy voice made everything in her body respond. She liked him this way. Raw and fierce. Here was the man he kept hidden, and he was going to share that with her.

And she wanted to be the woman that could handle it. Not just for him, but for herself. All the time she was struggling to find who she was, show people she was more, yet he treated her like she already was more. Treated her like she was strong.

She loved the idea of being taken over by him. Being his. Giving up the competition, challenging him but letting him win her however he wanted. There was something freeing and sexy and strengthening about that. And she wanted all of him.

"Okay," she whispered.

"Okay?" he said, mimicking her words. "Going to listen to me now?"

"Yes, sir," she said quickly.

What sounded like an approving groan broke through the air. "You want to touch me?"

"Yes, so much."

He pressed against her. She felt his powerful thighs hit the back of hers, his hips dig into her ass. Then she felt his hard, heavy cock rest in her bound palms at the small of her back.

"Oh…my…"

"Where's that mouth of yours? Don't tell me this—" he thrust against her, the velvety steel running along her palms "—is all it takes to bring you to heel."

She swallowed hard. She couldn't see him, but she could *feel* him, and man was he big. A flare of shock hit her. It had been so long since she had sex, and it had only been once. Could she and Sebastian even fit together?

"Say the word, Penny. You scared? Want me to stop?"

That was that moment her future hung on.

She replayed what he'd told her about himself. Trust. She had to trust him, and he had to trust her. She definitely wasn't ready to give up. Hell, they'd barely started. But she had to trust that they'd fit, that he'd make it work. He was the experienced one. People had sex all the time. Surely this would work.

Deep breath.

She'd trust him to make it work.

Instead of answering him, she closed her hands around him and gripped him.

He hissed and pumped his hips, fucking into her fists. He grew even harder. It was time to push the uncertainty away and go for it. This was what she'd been waiting for. To be with him, experience him completely and without inhibition. When he thrust again, she gripped him tighter. Though she had limited mobility, she rose to her tiptoes and tried angling him to her entrance. The tip barely breached her—

He pulled back, out of her grasp, and another slap came down on her ass.

He tsked. "I know you're eager, but this goes at my pace." He palmed her ass again. She heard movement behind her and then, sweet Jesus, his mouth was on her heat.

"Oh, God, yes." She sighed, and her whole body relaxed, letting the table completely support her weight—her legs turning to little better than jelly.

He was on his knees, mouth between her legs, and nothing ever felt better.

"You're wet," he said, trailing his tongue along her slit. "Wet just from the spanking." He buried his tongue deep and she moaned. "You like getting your ass slapped?"

She arched further and nodded. Words were too difficult to come up with in that moment. And when he stopped, she whined, "No, no don't stop."

"Then answer me."

"Yes," she groaned. "I like you spanking me. It's…a mix of things."

"Mix?" He returned his mouth, licking her clit, then sucking on it. She forgot how to speak, but when he started to pull away again, she found her voice real quick. Anything to get him to stay.

"Y-yes, a mix of feelings. It hurts, but it also feels good. I…I can't explain it. I just like…"

When his tongue covered her entire sex, drinking her down and rubbing every nerve ending, she was on the brink of coming.

"What do you like?" he rasped against her hot flesh.

"I like how you take me over," she said.

It was the honest truth, and once she said it, everything

made more sense. She wanted to be strong, wanted to be a woman that knew herself and had experience, but she wanted to belong. Belong to him. Because he made her feel seen, wanted, needed, crazed. All of it wrapped up into their banter, their connection, their completion. It all lead to this. The moment of feeling totally taken over while feeling stronger than she'd ever felt. *How* exactly he brought that out in her, she still wasn't sure.

"I like taking you over," he said, sliding one finger inside her sheath. He pumped in and out a few times, then added another finger.

"Fuck," he whispered. "You're tight, darlin'. I wanted to wait. To make you come around my cock—"

"I want that!" she shot out, terrified he was prepping to leave her.

A low chuckle came, and the sound gave her goose bumps.

"I want that, too. But I need you soaking for that. Otherwise it won't feel as good." With two fingers buried deep, his mouth returned to suck her clit.

"Oh!" she cried, her breath fanning over the table. She let him pleasure her body like he owned it. Because in that moment, he did.

No one knew her body like him. Not even herself. An impressive feat considering they were still at the beginning of their "two-week exploration program."

But he cared about her pleasure. Cared about her body. She'd been right to trust him. Whether he knew by her pause when she felt his cock for the first time or just assumed she'd need extra preparation, he was taking care of her. And as her heart melted, her whole body followed.

Every muscle tensed as he stirred his fingers in and out,

the glide of that thickness disappearing inside her slickened more with her arousal. He flicked his tongue over her clit while fucking her with his hand. Over and over. A steady pace that kept her on edge and drowned her in bliss. It was a tortuous ecstasy, and she needed to come.

"I'm wet, I promise," she said. She was ready for more. His fingers no longer enough. She wanted him. All of him.

"I know you are, darlin'. You're doing so well." He pumped again and again. "I still need more though."

"Please," she whispered, her bound wrists fidgeting. Damn it, she needed him so bad. Needed him to fill her body, to take her wild and hard and entirely until they both couldn't breathe. The teasing was becoming too much. "Do you have any idea what you're doing to me?"

"Yes." He rose, pulled away from her body, and moved so she could see his face. He raised his fingers, the ones that had just been inside of her. They were glistening.

He smiled and met her stare. "I'm doing this to you." He licked his fingertip, then with a sexy grin, went back behind her.

He was in control. She knew, and so did he. Working her body and preparing her exactly the way he wanted.

All she could do was stand there, bent over, and take it.

"I need you to give up more," he said, thrusting those two fingers into her again with an easy glide. But he kept them deep and rubbed the spot inside while he licked madly at her clit.

As if a dam burst, she came hard and fast.

"There it is," he rasped against her and kept licking.

She screamed his name. Before her orgasm was even finished rushing through her, he pulled away, and she heard the rip of cellophane.

"That's my girl," he said, his palm cupping between her legs, as if to gather moisture. She was panting, her body still contracting from the aftershocks of an orgasm that was half fulfilled.

She peeled her eyes open and looked over her shoulder to catch of glimpse of him.

He was rubbing his cock, coating the condom with her cream. Though it was dark and she could only make out shadows, the sight of him using what he'd wrought from her on himself was the sexiest thing she'd ever seen.

He kicked her heels apart, spreading her wider. The tip of his cock met her weeping entrance and she breathed deep, desperate for this moment. Her skin was buzzing, her core aching and empty.

"You are so fucking beautiful," he rasped. "And tonight, you're all mine."

He thrust hard, sinking himself all the way to the hilt. A slice of shock, lust, and just a hint of pain raced through her like a bullet.

"Fuck!" he growled. "So perfect."

He stirred his hips, and she gasped. He was thick, long, and hit every single nerve she had.

"You understand now?" he asked, as if he was on the brink of control himself. "You're drenched, taking all of me, and still so fucking tight."

Yes, he was right. Prepping her was a good thing, because even with her soaked from an orgasm, it was till a tight fit. But nothing felt more right. More amazing.

He withdrew completely. Cold air whooshed over her heated flesh, and she lost her mind. Was ready to beg.

"Come back!" She struggled against her bounds and went to move to him, to chase him down if she had to, but his palm landed heavy on her neck, keeping her bent over the table.

"Tell me," he said, sliding his cock along her folds, and she sighed with contentment. He was still there. Now if only she could get him back inside. "Tell me what you want."

"You," she said.

"How?" He rubbed that thick length along her again. "I want to hear you say how you want me."

"Deep," she murmured.

"Details," he countered, continuing his teasing. He was so close, right there, but not breeching. "What do you want deep? What does this pretty pussy want?"

A jolt of lust raced at his words. He was making her say it. Waking up her body and her mind. Forcing her to voice what she wanted. He made her feel like it was okay to say such things.

"I want your cock. Hard...deep..." She wiggled her bottom. "I want to come. Want to scream. I want..." And the truth hit her, what she was trying to explain earlier. "I want you to fuck me until the pleasure is so much it borders on pain."

Because that's where she'd been for years. On the brink of pain from wanting him.

"You surprise me," he mumbled, so soft she barely heard it. But he sounded...amazed? As if they'd connected in a way he hadn't expected.

"Trust," he said. "Remember what I said about that?"

"Yes," she said. "You're trusting me to tell you the truth. I am."

"Then I'm going to give you what you asked for."

He surged inside her once more, the action pushing her forward.

"Yes! Sebastian, yes!"

This was what she needed. *He* was who she needed.

He wrapped one arm around her waist, shielding her stomach from banging against the edge of the table, and pulled her closer.

She could barely keep her toes on the floor, because with every inward thrust, he pulled her back against him, fucking her deep. But he didn't stop.

"You want hard, darlin'?" His hips slammed against her ass as he took her.

"Yes." It was a whimper, because her body was spiraling out of control. Between the last orgasm and the coming one, she was kept in a constant state of edgy pleasure.

With his free hand, he grabbed her bound wrists, using them as leverage to push himself even deeper. He fucked her as promised, harder, faster, and all she could do was try to breathe and hold on for dear life.

She didn't think it was possible to be that consumed. That overwhelmed and overtaken. His cock effortlessly slid over that sensitive spot inside her. Instead of his fingers rubbing, it was the crown of his cock sliding along it, over and over.

Her body burned from the inside out. But she needed more. She felt full, fuller than she could handle, and still it wasn't enough.

She chanced the one word she'd been scared to say. "More."

He stopped, seated deep inside, hands gripping her.

She didn't know what he'd do next, but she knew there was more to be had. More that he was still holding out on.

Just...more.

And she wanted it.

He withdrew and cupped her hips, turning her to face him. Without a beat, he lifted her onto the table, the glossy wood beneath her bare ass warm from where her body had been bent over it.

"More?" he asked, confirming if he'd heard her right.

Her mouth went dry because, though it was dark, moonlight cast faint shadows over the man before her, and he was incredible. His strong chest looked chiseled from stone. His abs were so cut and defined that every time he took a breath, they flexed a little more, and she reached for—

But she stopped short. Her hands were bound behind her back. No matter how hard she tried, she couldn't reach for him. Couldn't touch him. She could barely see him.

"I asked you a question."

She met his eyes. "Yes. More." So much more. She wanted to touch him, taste him, feel him. He'd been deep inside of her body, yet still, he hadn't kissed her. She wasn't able to hug him to her. Yes, she wanted so much more. She wanted it all.

Getting a handle on her trembling body, she tested her confidence and spread her legs, coaxing him back to her.

He palmed the tops of her thighs, gently massaging them, and stared at her. Then, he spread her legs wider.

She gasped, but he stepped between her legs and yanked her close. His cock instantly surged inside her. Her head fell back, and she moaned. She didn't think she'd ever get enough of him.

"You want deeper, harder?" he rasped, pumping twice, three times, pausing only to lean over her to suck a nipple between his teeth until he had her whole body crackling with pleasure. "Then lay back."

She did as she was told. Lying down with her hands behind her wasn't very comfortable, but it made her back arch and put her breasts on display. Any discomfort was worth the hungry look in his eyes as his glance caressed her body.

"Be careful what you ask for, darlin'." His voice was dangerously low as he slid his hands to her ankles and lifted both legs.

Her eyes went wide as she watched him rest her heels on the top of his shoulders, on either side of his head.

Still inside of her, he said nothing else. Just hugged her thighs and grinned like he was in on some secret she wasn't aware of. His eyes were fused to her.

"Deeper," he said, as if answering her command, and thrust.

She screamed and arched further. She didn't think it was possible. He was already buried to the hilt, yet now, with the backs of her legs against his chest, he pumped another inch inside her body.

"Harder," he said, retreating and thrusting with all his might back inside her. Again, delivering on her request. His hold on her thighs tightened as he hugged them the way he might a person.

He did this, again and again. Fucking her so hard and deep that a sheen of sweat broke over his skin. Her breasts bounced violently as he surged in and out so hard and fast, she couldn't breathe. She could only take it.

She was so mindless, she hadn't even realized she was coming until a white light blazed across her vision and her entire body tensed as her inner walls spasmed.

"Good girl," he praised. "You're a good girl, but I know better now. You like this, don't you? Your tight little pussy likes being fucked hard, doesn't it?"

"Yes!" she cried to the ceiling, her toes curling and her body shuddering from the pleasure. It didn't stop, because he didn't stop. He fucked her though her orgasm until she was on the brink of another one.

He kissed her inner knee, then bit down. "You're going to make me come. But I want one more from you. Come on, make it hurt. Make it so good it hurts."

She tried to tell him yes. Tried to say that it was so good it hurt. But she couldn't. All she could do was helplessly come once more. She was his prisoner as he invaded her body again and again.

"Fuck, yeah, that's my girl. Come all over me. Show me how much you like it."

With a strangled cry, she arched further, the lace digging into her wrists, her body shaking and sweating, her throat raw from screaming his name.

She didn't like it…she loved it.

Everything from his power to his strength to the way he spoke. He was an unleashed, dirty talking, no mercy lover that she wanted over and over.

He tensed against her and his cock grew impossibly harder. He came so hard that even with the barrier of a condom, she could feel him pulse and twitch from the intensity.

Breathing hard, he kept a tight hold of her legs and rested his forehead against her shin.

With the glow of their climaxes still clinging to them, she knew two things.

One, she could safely say Operation: Orgasm was a smashing success.

And two, she would have given anything for him to stay right there and never leave.

Chapter Six

Jesus Christ, what had he done?

Sebastian put two hands flat against the shower wall and hung his head. The shower spray hit him, but it didn't wash away his thoughts.

Penny was sleeping in her bed. After what he could only describe as the best sex of his life, he couldn't bring himself to leave. But he always left. Always.

Staying meant he A) actually wanted to continue to be near her, or B) had suffered a stroke and lost all ability to reason. His money was on the latter.

Staying with a woman… No, not just *a woman*. He was staying with Penelope Diamond. And he was there because something deep in his gut wanted to see her one more time before he snuck out. See those emerald eyes look up from those thick lashes. Maybe he'd get a sleepy smile.

Jesus…he had to get it together. This wasn't like him.

He'd untied her wrists, carried her to bed, and laid her

beneath the sheets. She was exhausted and had instantly fallen asleep. But the small upturn on her lips made him think she might be happy too.

An impossibility since he'd just ravaged her like some fucking animal.

And now, instead of hauling ass out of there, he was standing beneath the spray of the water, in her bathroom, and trying to get a grip. Because part of him was thinking of her smile and well-being, how staying would only jeopardize those things. But the other part was replaying the secret sexy vixen she was beneath the innocent façade. And God help him, he knew he had to have her again.

He'd taken her harder and rougher than anyone he'd ever had. And he'd gone on for…

"Hours," he murmured.

And yet she'd taken it, begged for it. Her tender body must be hurting and sore. Christ, she wasn't experienced, not even used to normal sex, much less to his kind of play. Truth be told, he'd lost himself in her.

It wasn't just the sex. It was her. Not how she let him handle her, but how *she* handled *him*. It was how she looked at him, arched for him. How she called out his name. How that sweet body just kept giving and taking. She'd given herself completely to him—he'd felt it.

And that was a heady drug he wanted another hit of.

The glass shower door slowly opened, and he looked over to find her standing perfectly naked and staring at him.

"Hi." Her voice was soft, and all that red hair was in wild tangles, hanging around her ivory skin. Fuck, she was gorgeous. She looked so innocent, so fragile.

He thought of what he'd just done to her an hour ago.

He really was a deviant.

"You okay?" It was the only thing he could ask. He saw a faint mark lining her wrists from where the lace had dug in. Her skin was flushed, her ass likely still pink.

"No. I'm not okay."

Shit. "I'm sorry."

He went to step out of the shower, to get as far away from her as possible and apologize for ever hurting her. But she placed her hands on his chest, stilling him. Instead of letting him step out, she maneuvered him back and stepped in.

His gaze stayed on her face. But hers? She looked from his eyes to his chest, down to his cock, which—damn the thing—was stirring already.

"You asked me what I wanted. Asked me to say it."

He nodded. He'd prepared himself for this moment. The one where she told him he was some kind of sadist in bed and he scared her and—

"I want to know you," she whispered.

The hands on his chest slowly moved down his stomach. She looked at him like he was some piece of art. She touched him, gliding her fingertips over every ridge of muscle and inch of skin. He felt an overwhelming sense of…peace.

She wanted to know him? The way she was touching him, looking at him, was like she was cherishing the sight and feel of something foreign. As if she didn't want to give him up.

For the next two weeks, he could only hope so. Eventually, they'd give each other up. But right now?

"Know me how?"

She smiled at him. "You've done a great job of showing me a thing or two." She laughed a little, but her hands brushed over his nipples, and he hissed. "But I want to learn how to make you feel good. I want to touch you, kiss you, like you touch and kiss me."

Temporary. A word he repeated in his mind to try to bring himself back to why things would never work out between them. Penny was light, Sebastian was dark, and long term was not in his DNA. He'd had a plan to push her away, showed her how rough he could be, thought last night would have done it.

But holy fucking hell. Not only was she *not* running the other way, she wanted more. Yet again. Only this time, in a very different way. This was either a dream or a nightmare, because no fucking way was he that lucky or that stupid to think this was a set up to fall really, really hard in the end.

He kept things on a surface, sexual level for a good reason. Hard and rough usually meant fucking, and that's what he did. Yet when he took her, it didn't matter how fast, or where they were, there was a deep sense of connection. Which was bad.

It took typically two weeks to form emotions that could mess with the surface dynamic he prided himself on keeping. That didn't seem to be the case with Penny. Which, again, was bad. The consequences were too great.

But with the way her soft hands were slowly sweeping over his chest, he could already see the temptation to fall into a spiral of bad decisions. Like wanting to know her right back, in a way that went much deeper than physically.

He should shut this down. The way she looked at him, touched him, was something he couldn't risk. Yes, he'd been wanted before, but in this way? It was like she had a true interest in him as a person. Had an interest in his pleasure as much as an interest in his life. He was all for teaching her a few lessons on sex, but her tenderness was blurring a line.

Shut this down.

He opened his mouth to tell her he was going to get out, dry off, and see her later. But instead, her mouth pressed against his chest, right over his heart, and a groan escaped. Those lush lips on his skin sent a shock of pulsing need through his entire body.

He'd kept things under control for a reason. He was realizing now that the moment her mouth hit him, he was a goner. Control was nowhere to be found.

No—he needed to keep his head. Keep this as simple as possible.

He maneuvered her under the spray of the water, hoping it'd help keep a distance.

Mistake.

While he might have broken the contact of her kissing his chest, he now stood before a drenched Penny Diamond, red hair falling like her own ruby waterfall around her creamy skin, beads of water trailing from her lips, to her breasts, and down her flat stomach.

"Is there any look you can't pull off, darlin'?" he rasped, drinking in the sight of how fucking amazing she was.

She glanced down at herself and smiled. "You like the wet look, huh?"

"I like you wet." He grinned. "That's no secret."

She laughed. "I suppose not."

She cupped his biceps and turned him to switch places with her so that the water hit his back and she was standing before him.

"This is my time now," she said, all joking gone. "I'm happy to give you what you want, but I want to feel you back."

She took a deep breath, and while she tried to look confident, he saw a slight tremble race over her as if she was nervous. "Let me?"

Then it hit him. She wasn't challenging him. Wasn't goading him on purpose. She was asking. Requesting to have free reign on his body.

The answer should be no.

And yet he found himself looking into those big green eyes that usually held so much fire and brazen, which now were heavy with passion and a little uncertainty, and found himself saying, "Okay."

She smiled, and he wanted to go to his knees just to keep that happiness on her face. But he was at her mercy now.

Part of him was curious. She was nothing if not a wild card. So he stood there, the hot water hitting his back and the shower steam enveloping them as she began to run her hands long his arms and up his shoulders.

"Your skin is really smooth," she said. "But you're hard beneath."

Her brows knit with concentration as she examined him. There was a constant state of appreciation and awe on her face. A look like that could do crazy things to a man's ego. So he stood still, letting her explore.

Had she really never gotten a chance to do this?

She'd had that jackass boyfriend, and he knew she wasn't experienced, but had she never really handled a man? Touched him intimately?

When her fingers dipped to his torso, tracing beads of water over various flanks of muscle, he wanted to sigh. It felt good. Her touch felt beyond good. It was like she was loving on him with just her hands and her gaze. Damn it felt nice.

Nice to be seen through her eyes.

When her hands reached the V of his hips, she pushed gently with her thumbs. She was relaxing him with her touch.

"Yikes," she said, her eyes fused to his cock, which was hard as steel and ready to go.

He chuckled. "Yikes?"

She looked up and nodded. "You are," she glanced down, "yikies."

Though he'd never heard a word quite like that, he'd take it as a compliment.

"Careful, darlin'. You may take my ego to new heights."

She smiled. "I felt it, I mean, I *really* felt it." Her cheeks blushed a little, and she met his eyes again. "But seeing it? Seeing you like this?" Her gaze swept over his entire body, and a surge of pride shot through him. "You're beautiful, Sebastian."

He cupped her face and frowned hard. This tiny woman had just made his whole chest hurt. The only thing he could do was lean in and kiss her.

She gasped against his mouth, which only made him want more. Slow and deep, he gently sucked her mouth between his, then delved his tongue inside. His question was finally answered: she tasted like strawberries everywhere.

She met his seeking tongue, taking aggressive laps at him like she was starved. There was nothing shy about her kiss. Wrapping her arms around his middle, she pulled herself closer, their wet skin sliding against each other. Her breasts pressed into his torso, collecting water between their bodies as drops fell around their faces.

He tilted her head and drove his tongue deeper. She was soft everywhere. Clinging to him, kissing him. Her sweet mouth parting, letting him in while dueling with his own. She was taking her pleasure from the kiss as she gave him his own.

Using his thumb, he brushed a water drop away from her cheek. Her lips lingered against his, both of them breathing deeply but not breaking contact.

"That," she said, "was our first kiss."

Holy shit, she was right. This whole time he'd been focused on keeping things surface, on teaching her about sex and using her body the way he needed, waiting for her to push him away, that he'd stayed away from kissing that perfect mouth.

Somehow, he knew kissing her would be a game changer.

Now he had to prove himself wrong. Kissing her, tasting those sweet lips, would be how he proved he could handle this. Handle her.

This is a fling. A short term deal.

But with a single brush, she snagged his mouth again, and nothing had ever felt so good. Damn if he didn't kiss her back. She trailed her lips to his neck and kissed his pulse, then lower, to his collarbone.

"There's still something you haven't taught me," she said as her mouth continued downward, delivering kisses along his hips to his bellybutton. She maneuvered him to sit on the bench along the back wall as she hit her knees before him.

He ran a hand through his hair, flicking the water back off of it, and looked down at her.

"I want to learn," she said and slid her hand up his chest, reaching for him. He clasped her wrist gently and massaged her palm. But when she reached further, running her fingertip along his lower lip while remaining on her knees, he struggled to find words.

"Show me," she said. Another sweep of her finger along

his mouth. "Show me what you like. Show me how."

Unable to deny her a damn thing, he snagged her fingertip between his teeth, then sucked it deep.

Keeping her eyes on him, she leaned in and gently scraped her teeth along the head of his cock, before sucking him deep in one long stroke.

"Fuck," he whispered, her finger falling from his mouth. She pulled away, still looking up at him. Waiting.

Oh, he caught on quick to this game. Problem was, he was usually the one in the driver's seat. While she might be on her knees, she was allowing him to keep his control. The sexy, smart woman currently had him wrapped around her finger. In every sense of the word.

"You've never sucked a man?" He wanted to clarify. He also wanted to hear her say—

"No. Just you."

That swell of pride was progressively growing. There was something sexy about her innocence and willingness. A gift she was giving him while taking everything he dished out. He wouldn't disappoint her.

Keeping his eyes on hers, he licked the tip of her finger, swirled his tongue around it, then sucked it quick.

She looked at his cock, then that sweet tongue darted out, tasting the head, circling the crown, then she sucked the tip hard before letting it pop from her mouth.

She'd done just as he'd shown her, and damn was she a good student. Her mouth closing over his cock was the second best thing he'd ever felt, right behind being inside her when she came.

When that green gaze hit his, as if awaiting the next instructions, he struggled not to come right then.

He took her finger deep and sucked hard. She gasped, and her eyes widened. Then he slowly released it, sucking as he went back up the digit until it slid from his mouth.

How deep could she go?

She licked her lips, closed her mouth over his cock, and sucked him down.

Shit, no amount of effort would keep him from coming soon. Her lack of experience didn't matter. She was too good. His eyes slid closed as he relished the feel of her hot mouth surrounding him.

She moaned, the vibrations shooting from his dick to his spine and making it even more difficult to hold out.

He looked down at her. Her auburn brows were furrowed, her free hand on his thigh, nails just starting to dig in. She tried to go deeper but moaned again when she gained no ground.

With a frustrated sigh, she eased up and sat back on her haunches, looking at his cock like a mountain she couldn't scale to the top.

"I can't," she said.

He cupped her face and shook his head, trying not to laugh. "Darlin', this," he gestured at his raging cock, which was so hard he was almost in agony, "is not failing. You make me feel so good."

"But I can't go deep."

"It's okay."

"It's not okay," she shot out. "There's got to be a way. I know you're big, but I can go deeper than that, can't I?"

"Darlin,' you're doing great. You don't need to go deeper."

"I want to. I thought you were supposed to teach me

things." There was that challenge in her voice. The gentle Penny was gone, replaced by the one who liked competition just as much as he did.

"You sure about this?" He stood and, with his palms still cupping her face, coaxed her back to his cock until the tip prodded her lips. She instantly parted for him, and he stifled a groan.

"First, you need to follow your instinct. Do what feels good."

She looked up and him and hummed.

He smiled. "Trust me, whatever makes you feel good will make me feel good. It's about giving into the passion and pleasure."

With the head of his cock in her mouth, she huffed but gave in to what he was saying.

"Now," he said, angling her face up so her neck was long and smooth. "Relax your throat, your lungs, your whole body."

She nodded and closed her eyes for a moment.

"Good girl. I can feel that, you know? I'm not even completely buried in that sweet mouth of yours, and I can feel already the tension leaving you."

She smiled a little, the sight nearly his undoing. Penny Diamond on her knees, the head of his cock bobbing in her mouth, and her smiling like it was a damn treat? Fuck, he was going to go off like a damn teenager before they really got started.

Focus.

He took his own deep breath and continued.

"Now, keep your eyes on mine. And keep your neck," he ran the back of his finger along her throat, "long like this. It will help."

She did, and he went back to holding her face like a treasure between his hands. Because she was, and goddamn it, he was fighting every instinct not to fuck her mouth hard. No, he had to go slow.

"I'm going to help you take it, understand."

She nodded.

"Deep breath in."

She did.

"And out."

When she exhaled, he pushed deep in a measured thrust, hitting the back of her throat, then retreated.

Her eyes went wide, and she smiled again. Which made him smile. "See?" He caressed her cheek. "You did so well. You didn't fail."

"Again," she said in a muffled tone around his cock.

He raised a brow. "What have I warned you about being careful what you ask for?" He felt the gentle scrape of her teeth. "Oh, that's how you want to play?"

She nodded and said, "Again!" in a forceful tone with a mouthful of him.

He'd never been so fucking hard and turned on in his life. She was a damn wanton. Looked like the all-American good girl. And the moment she was bent over or on her knees, she was anything but.

She was his.

For that moment at least.

And he would give her what she wanted.

He surged deep again, then withdrew. She moaned, and when he did it again, she bobbed back, taking him a fraction deeper.

"Fuck, you're going to make me come already."

Holding her face, he fucked her sweet mouth slowly, and she took it. Not only took it, but moaned and clawed at him for more. She grabbed his ass, her finger nails sinking in as she pulled him closer. The sting of pain mixed with her eager sucking was too much and he couldn't last.

"Pull back, darlin'. I'm going to come."

She didn't. She sank her nails in deeper and he yelled to the ceiling as hot jets shot forth. She kept sucking, drinking him down like he was her lifeline.

His entire body shuddered, the intensity of his release almost toppling him over.

She slowly released him. He instantly hit his knees, breathing hard and facing her.

"Do you ever do anything I expect?"

She smiled. "What would be the fun in that?"

He kissed her hard, laying her back in the tub, the shower raining over them. Considering how sore she likely was, he didn't want to push her, but he needed to feel her come, make her feel what she'd just made him feel.

"Bass?" she asked, but he was too busy to answer questions.

He kissed down her body, sucking her nipples hard until she arched and moaned. The damn tub wasn't big enough for him to get between her legs like he wanted, so he sat up and moved just enough that the water pelted her breasts.

Her nipples strained to tighter points from the lashes of water hitting them. Her wet hair splayed over the edge of the tub, and he spread her legs as wide as he could and rubbed her clit.

"Oh God!"

She was wet, and not from the water. Her pussy was drenched. Was it all just from sucking him off? Though he'd just come, the thought made his cock stir. Something about this woman had him thinking he might never get enough.

A terrifying notion, one he pushed aside. Because he had other things to think about, like Penny laid out before him. His prize. A prize he was going to take.

Using two fingers, he rubbed fast over her sensitive bundle of nerves and watched her arch and moan. The water hitting her breasts, her thrashing and licking her lips while he took her over the edge.

"Yes!" she cried out.

Her whole body tensed, and it took all the will power he had not to thrust his fingers inside and feel her come. But he kept them on her clit and watched her fall apart.

When her eyes opened slowly and fastened on his face, she smiled. Those two delicate arms reached out for him, and damn if he didn't have a clue what to do. Because for the first time, he desperately wanted to reach back.

Chapter Seven

"Whose balls do you like better? Mine or Colts?" Huck asked.

Bass crossed his arms and shook his head. Standing in the middle of Sam's Sporting Goods Store, Huck held up two basketballs while Colt showed his six-year-old nephew Alex other options.

"You're an idiot," Sebastian said, but he couldn't help smiling a little. Huck had a way of always bringing out the humor in a situation. Which was nice since Sebastian hadn't been feeling overly humorous since he'd left Penny last night.

She'd rocked his world. Not in a simple sex kind of way, but in a weird way that left his chest sore. As if she'd reached in and clenched his heart.

"Why am I even here?" Sebastian asked, checking his watch.

It was Tuesday, and he had a late afternoon meeting starting soon. The only reason he'd come to Sam's was because the mom and pop store was only a few blocks away from his office.

"Because you've been ditching us and kind of a douche lately," Colt said over his shoulder. "Alex starts biddy-ball next week, and you're the one with the basketball skills." He handed Alex a small-sized basketball to try out.

Bass wouldn't say he was an expert. While all of them had played some kind of ball in high school, he had played basketball in college, and to this day, throwing the ball up, banking some shots in his driveway, was how he de-stressed.

"What's a douche?" Alex asked, bouncing the ball twice before it hit his foot and rolled to down the aisle.

"Good luck explaining to Lily why her son now knows the word douche," Bass said.

Colt just shrugged and wrangled the ball for Alex.

"Uncle Bass is just being grouchy. Grouchy and douchey are kind of the same thing, but let's not say that word, okay?"

"Is it a bad word?"

"Yeah…" Colt said. "Your mama would have my ass if she heard you say it."

"Ass is a bad word too, Uncle Colt."

"I think it's best you just don't pay attention to your Uncle Colt, kiddo," Bass said. He grabbed a size five ball from the top shelf and handed it to Alex. "Try this size."

Alex bounced it. "I like it!" He bounced it a few more times.

"Alex should ignore me, but *you* should listen," Colt said to Bass. "Do you have a date for the wedding?"

"I don't date," Bass said in a bored tone.

"Yes you do, you just don't date consecutively. But since you don't have someone lined up, Jenna's friend is coming in to be her third bridesmaid—"

"And you and Jenna have gone into the matchmaking business?"

"Come on, she's not going to know anyone, and she's staying at our place while we're honeymooning."

Bass exhaled. He didn't mind showing the woman around or being a friendly face. Actually, it would be smart to set up some kind of date for the wedding itself. Yes, the last day of his and Penny's arrangement was the rehearsal dinner, but come the wedding the next day, they'd be done with their secret fling.

"I can tell you're thinking about it." Colt grinned.

"Why are you so interested in me dating or not?"

"At some point it would be good to see you settling...or at least moving in that direction."

"Says the man who rode the circuit and hopped from town to town for how long?"

"Yeah, that was what I did. And it got old. I'm just saying, it's nice having someone that really gets you, you know?"

No, Bass didn't know. But it was all his buddy talked about since he and Jenna had gotten serious. He'd spent the last several months watching his engaged friends giggle and swoon and even make out every damn time the other one was within arm's reach.

If he were being honest, which he wasn't, a small part of him might admit that he wasn't jealous of his friends, he was envious. Of course, that small part got stomped out by his better logic, reminding him why he kept things short term. So short term that the only person who'd come close to really understanding him was Penny. A revelation that both intrigued and terrified him.

"This is hard," Alex said, getting Bass out of that conversation. Thank God.

"Yeah, but you'll learn," Bass said. "Sometimes things that are difficult, like basketball, turn out to be the things you enjoy the most."

The minute Bass said the words he wasn't thinking of basketball, he thought of Penny. She could be the sexiest pain in the ass he'd ever encountered, but there he was, thinking of nothing but getting back in her presence.

"I meant that it's hard keeping track of words. Especially bad words," Alex said, clarifying his earlier statement as he concentrated on bouncing the basketball. "What if I forget what's good and bad words? There's a lot of words, you know?"

Bass nodded. "Yeah, I know, kiddo."

"I don't want to mess up and get Uncle Colt in trouble by saying a bad one."

He looked around. Where the hell were Colt and Huck? After scanning the store, he saw Colt looking at little kid high-tops and Huck "testing" out the weights by lifting them.

Ah shit, he was alone with the kid, standing in the middle of a sporting goods store, trying to explain words?

Great...

"Here's what I do. When someone asks you a question, and you're not sure what to say or have the right words, just say 'define' and repeat what they asked you."

Alex stopped dribbling, grabbed the ball, and looked at him. "What does that do?"

He shrugged. "It buys you time to think of something else." It was a trick he used in the court room. Besides, clear expectations and agreements were a must. Which was why he liked everything in black and white.

His mind flashed again to Penny and all the gray she was putting in his world.

Was gray so bad? He could live with a little more excitement than he was used to. The boundaries were still in place. He was safe.

Just because he enjoyed what they were doing didn't mean he was all emotional or feeling shit. Of course he enjoyed her. Hell, he was living out a fantasy he'd long thought was never going to happen. But that didn't mean everything had to fall apart now, not when they were having so much fun. They had an agreement. Two weeks, purely sex. He would teach her things, then go back to being friends.

She was going to fuck someone anyway, may as well have been me.

Yeah, too bad that excuse wasn't helping him sleep at night when thinking of lying to Ryder about this situation. It also wasn't helping when he thought of Penny as much more than a fling. Those were the kind of thoughts he needed to get under control ASAP.

"You're smart, Uncle Bass." Alex smiled.

He wanted to laugh. He didn't feel smart. He felt like a fucking moron, actually. But he'd take the compliment.

"Thanks, kid. You're pretty smart too. And a promising basketball player."

Alex dribbled down the aisle just as Colt came up with shoes in hand. "These are good shoes for basketball, right?"

Bass looked at them. "Those are track shoes. You want high tops that support the ankle."

Colt looked at the pair in his hand, mumbled something like, "Ah, hell," and went back to the wall of shoes.

Seeing Colt spend time with his nephew and being back home made life feel like it was coming together. But watching the one time Rodeo Romeo settle down, shop for kid shoes, and plan a wedding, all while maintaining a stupid ass smile on his face 24/7 from the bliss he felt, that was cool. He was happy for his friend.

No matter how happy he was for Colt though, he had to remind himself that kind of life wasn't for him.

He had no problem with responsibility, he had a problem with the emotional attachment. Trust was one thing. It was something you could trade with a lover, a friend, and hope for the best in terms of an equal exchange. But taking it further? Counting on someone to love you and want you above all others? Want you enough to stay and commit to long term and never leave?

No. Life had more than taught him those things weren't in the cards for him. Sebastian's own mother had left him. His own fucking mother. How someone could leave their child was beyond him. Which was why he was never going to have one. Or a wife for that matter. He'd seen what a woman could do to a man simply by walking out.

No fucking way was that ever going to be him.

"Hey!" Lily called as the bell to the front of the shop opened. Decked out in scrubs with giraffes on them, she'd come straight from work. Clutching her purse, she made her way toward Alex.

"Mama, look!" He dribbled a couple of times with a big smile on his face.

"Aw, you're a star, honey."

"And I found some shoes," Colt said, walking up with a pair of actual basketball shoes.

"Thank you guys for helping me with this. His first game is tomorrow, and I haven't had time to get him here after school."

"We're happy to help, Lil," Colt said.

"Yeah," Sebastian agreed. "Though Huck over there is helping his biceps, so you may want to rein him in."

Lily laughed. "Yeah, well we better get going, honey." Lily frowned, looking at Alex. "Is that chocolate on your mouth?"

Alex's eyes went just about as wide as Colt's. Shit. They were both busted from the ice cream cones they'd had earlier.

"Alex McCade, did you spoil your dinner by having sweets?"

Alex glanced at him, then looked his mother dead in the eye. "Define: *having sweets*."

Lily's brows shot up, and both Bass and Colt laughed.

"Great." She sighed and looked at Bass. "Don't think I don't know where he got that from, Mr. Attorney."

With that, they headed toward the register, but not before Colt slapped his back. "You're pretty good with this kid stuff. Thanks for your help, buddy."

His throat closed a little.

He needed a beer and a heavy dose of reality. Because what had happened over the last twenty-four hours was not only *not* standard, it was unobtainable. It was one thing to see his friends get a shot at lifelong happiness. One thing to allow himself to envy them. But to think he could have those things? To for a moment wonder if he was even capable of them?

He was good at short term.

It was best he remembered that.

• • •

Penny grabbed some baker's chocolate off the shelf and placed it in her basket. To tell the truth, she was glad to do a little grocery shopping. Maybe it would help her come back down to earth for a minute, help her stop thinking about Bass and the fact that he had left after their shower last night. There were other things in the world, right?

Like her plans with Jenna. Jenna was stopping by tonight to sample some desserts Penny was making for the rehearsal dinner.

She glanced at her shopping list—

"Chocolate, whip cream, and strawberries," a gruff voice said from behind her. "Looks like a fun night to me."

She turned to find Sebastian, his own basket in hand, looking at her with those knee-weakening dark eyes.

"Not as fun as you'd think. I'm baking."

He nodded, and she took the opportunity to examine the contents of his basket.

"Frozen dinner, beer, and protein bars?" she asked.

He shrugged. "Why do you think I eat at your restaurant so much? Cooking isn't one of my strengths."

"Well, you have many other strengths," she said, grinning and tucking a lock of hair behind her ear. God, she felt like a flirting teenager reliving the events from last night.

"About that," he said, the tone of his voice turning the conversation in a direction that sounded serious. "Are you—"

"Hey guys!" Huck said, walking up to them. Penny instantly took a step away from Sebastian, as if they had just been caught doing something naughty. How risqué could she be in the baking aisle though?

But if the way her skin flushed just standing next to Bass was any indication, things could get pretty intense without them doing anything at all. She didn't even have to touch him to feel the impact he had. The mere thought of him, his closeness, how he looked at her, made her entire body hum with anticipation.

"Hi," she greeted Huck, finally able to get some words out. "Funny running into both of you here."

"We were just across the street, helping Alex with a basketball crisis," Bass said, then glanced at Huck. "Well, some of us were helping. Others were concerned with their biceps."

"Hey, I was testing the equipment," Huck said with a smile, flexing the bicep in question. "Don't worry, the weights work really well."

Penny laughed. "Good to know."

"So what are you two doing?" Huck asked, looking between her and Bass.

"I was just getting the last thing I needed and heading home," she said.

"What's the last thing?" Sebastian asked.

"Vodka."

Huck looked in her basket and smiled. Sebastian, however, kept his eyes on hers.

"Judging by your items there, looks like you're having a party," Huck said.

"Party of one mostly. I'm making some desserts for Jenna to try later. I put vodka in the pie crust. Makes it flakier."

"Awesome, well I'll see you at the checkout then," Huck said. Penny followed in the same direction.

"Penny," Sebastian called after her in a low tone. She turned to face him. "I'll see you later."

She nodded. She didn't know what later meant in Sebastian-speak. Could be tomorrow, a week from now, who knew. But she loved the idea that it would happen.

"Well you know where to find me." She looked at her basket, then at him. "Whip cream and all."

· · ·

"These tarts are great," Jenna said, taking a bite of one of the many desserts Penny had made.

"I was thinking we could do a few mini desserts at the rehearsal dinner to keep it lighter and give more options."

"I love it!" Jenna said, shoving the rest of the tart in her mouth.

Penny's kitchen was a disaster, and it was pushing nine p.m., but baking samples for Jenna had finally given her mind something to focus on other than the memory of Bass staring her down at the grocery store today.

"Oh my God, are these tiny chocolate cream pies?" Jenna took one and shoved the whole thing in her mouth. A resounding "*mmmm*" followed. She nodded and gave a thumbs up while she processed the massive bite.

"Well I'm glad you like all this. I was thinking of putting out trays of the various kinds of desserts at each table after dinner. Then people can pick and choose."

Jenna swallowed the rest of her bite. "Love it even more! Speaking of the rehearsal dinner, do you have a date for it?"

"No. Figured I'd be pretty busy overseeing the dinner and—"

"You said you have staff for that. You're in the wedding party. I want you to have fun."

"I will. I'll just be in the background, making sure the food is prepped and getting out and all that."

"As long as you actually interact with us and don't spend all night behind the bar."

"I won't."

"Good, so a date then. You still need one."

"I didn't say that. I'm just going to hang with Lily and the guys."

"They all have dates," Jenna said, like Penny was an idiot for not knowing such a thing.

"Everyone?"

Jenna nodded. "Except for Huck."

"Really? He's usually the first one to have a date."

"I know. But I think something is going on with him. Anyway, I'm surprised Ryder didn't tell you. He met some woman when he was in Wichita, and I guess she's coming in."

"Right…Ryder." Her brother was the least of her concerns at the moment. Granted, he seemed to think he had a right to weigh in on her dating life, then apparently could just do what he wanted. Not that she would have thrown a fit. She loved her brother and wanted him to be happy. But everyone had a date? Did that mean…

"So Bass has a date?"

Jenna shrugged like it was her life mission to play matchmaker. "Colt was talking to Bass today, and he seemed interested in going with my friend who's coming from out of town and housesitting while Colt and I are going on our honeymoon."

She swallowed hard and tried not to let the burning in her gut flare up. The rehearsal dinner was their last day together. And she was looking forward to every hour she had with Bass. They might not be going to the rehearsal "together," but he'd said it himself. Until the two weeks were up, she was his, and he was hers.

Mine.

She wanted her full two weeks, damn it. Down to the final minute. Was this what he'd tried to tell her earlier at the store?

"Isn't this friend of yours the same one that's the third bridesmaid?"

Jenna nodded. None of them had met her, but apparently this woman and Jenna were friends from college. She wondered if this woman was pretty. Would she like Bass? Of course she would, he was sinful and sexy and...

A sick ache twisted in her gut thinking of him with someone else. Not only that, but he was already making plans to replace her. He'd made it clear that they were a two week deal, then back to friends. And she'd agreed.

So why did the idea that he was making plans with someone else bother her like it did? Even if they wanted to go to the rehearsal dinner together, they couldn't. Right? Unless she pushed for that. Revisited the "terms of the agreement" and saw if there was wiggle room with his two-week only stance. Why would she even try and risk the rejection though?

Because I like him.

She always had. This wasn't breaking news. But at some point over the past few days, she'd begun to think he could be more.

To think *they* could be more.

Of course, now she knew he already had another date set up for as soon as their arrangement ended. That pretty much clinched the impossibility of extending this beyond two weeks.

I guess I was wrong.

It was sex. Temporary.

"You okay?" Jenna asked.

"Yeah." Penny looked around her kitchen, then down the front of her flour-stained jeans and tank top. "I was just going to start cleaning up here and get ready for bed. Long day."

"Oh, okay. Well everything is delicious, and thank you so much for helping with the dinner. I really appreciate it."

Jenna hugged her and left. Penny looked at the various fudge, puddings, and pie fillings and blew a lock of hair out of her eyes.

Funny how today could go from awesome to a big fat mess in no time.

Chapter Eight

Penny hadn't even dug into the dishes when a knock came at her door. She thought it was Jenna coming back, but she was greeted by a tall, dark, and handsome attorney instead.

She gripped the doorframe.

"Can I help you?" The words were harsher than she'd meant.

"Can I come in? I need to talk to you."

"Oh? Whatever about?"

He frowned at her. "About last night."

Ah yes, he had started saying something about that earlier at the grocery store.

"I was a bit rough and wanted to make sure you were okay," he said.

She opened the door, and he walked in. She went immediately to the kitchen to start on the dishes.

"I'm fine," she said. "Besides, you said you liked it rough. Turns out, so do I. So don't worry about it."

"Penelope." His voice was soft, and his hands cupped her waist from behind. "I never meant to hurt you. If I did—"

"I'm fine." She spun to face him. "You think city girls are the only ones who can handle you?" She scoffed. "I may not look the part, but trust me, what you dished out last night was nothing I couldn't handle."

"Then why are you upset?"

"I'm tired. You know." She gestured at the kitchen. "Baking and working today, only to have my friend come tell me that I need a date for the rehearsal dinner because everyone else has one."

His eyes narrowed. "Is that so?"

"Yeah. You could have just told me. I know our little agreement has an expatriation, but I never took you for an over-lapper. You didn't have to hide it."

"I'm not hiding anything. I don't have a date for the dinner per say."

She paused. "But Jenna said that Colt said—"

"Well that sounds like a good string of logic." He stepped toward her. "Colt and Jenna want me to occupy—"

"The third bridesmaid. I know. Jenna was gushing about setting you two up."

"You could have just asked me. This whole thing we have is supposed to be built on trust."

"Temporary trust," she mumbled.

He stood still, a mask of some dark emotion on his face. Anger? Disappointment? She couldn't tell.

"Are you setting up a date with someone else *the day* our time is up?" she asked. That's what he'd said he wanted, for her to just come out and ask.

"You're the one who came after me. Wanted something

from me. I was honest from the beginning, and you agreed to the timeline."

"Yes, you were honest," she said. Yet somehow it didn't make the ache in her stomach any less. She was falling for him. Hell, had fallen a long time ago. Now she was just falling faster. It was her own fault. Going against the guidelines they'd set up.

Bass ran the back of his fingers along her cheek, and she looked up at him. He opened his mouth to say something, then snapped it shut.

"I'll see you later," he said. But there was a flicker of longing behind his eyes. Was there hope? Could the self-proclaimed bachelor for life maybe want more? Was it possible he was just afraid? Just needed someone to show him it was worth taking that single step outside his boundaries?

She hoped so, because now more than ever, she knew that's what she wanted.

So why not go for it? She had just over a week left with him. If she was feeling something for him already, maybe he wasn't completely immune to her. It was only when she'd pushed him that he'd let his true self out. And she liked that man. Wanted him.

If I want him, I have to push for more.

What did she have to lose? If she did nothing, he would walk away in two weeks anyway. Hurt now or hurt later. Or maybe prove to him that there was more between them than sex.

It was worth a try. This whole situation had started because she'd finally gone after something she wanted. And she wasn't about to give up now.

A week and a half…could she show Bass that long term

beyond that might not be so bad?

She'd sure as hell try.

Because the idea of someone else didn't feel right. It felt depressing.

This was going to be the biggest challenge yet.

"You could stay," she said.

He stopped by her door. "No, I can't."

"Why?"

He laughed and glanced down. "You don't want to know."

"I wouldn't ask if I didn't."

His dark eyes met hers. "Because if I stay, I'll fuck you. And I'm not prepared for that. It wasn't why I came over. Actually, I wasn't even going to stop by tonight."

"But you did."

"Yeah, and now I'm going."

"What do you mean prepared? What, you have to do pushups beforehand? Guzzle down a protein shake or something?"

He glared at her, and she put her hands on her hips and raised her eyebrows, waiting for a response. Yeah, she was pretty certain she was the only person in his life that pushed him. Pushed for the truth. Pushed for his affection. Pushed for his trust.

"I don't have condoms on me. That's what I mean by prepared."

Oh. What went through her mind made it to her mouth and out loud before she could call it back.

"I was only with one man, one time before you, and we used a condom. I still got checked, just for precaution, so... I'm healthy, if that's your concern."

She glanced at her feet, because his dark stare was too

heavy to take. Since she'd put that out there, she may as well go the rest of the way.

"I'm on birth control, too." When he just stood there, she went on, shrugging and hating how pathetic she felt. "I was hoping that someday, when I was with a man I trusted, *I'd* be prepared. I just didn't know when that someday was."

She'd never admitted that because it sounded lame. Like she was waiting around for prince charming to come sweep her off her feet and carry her to her castle with a white picket fence.

But she'd hoped that one day Mr. Right would show up. And there, standing before Sebastian, it hit her. Deep down, she'd always hoped it would be him.

Now I really sound like an idiot.

"Well…" He cleared his throat. "I've never been with a woman without a condom."

Her eyes shot to his. "Never?"

He shook his head. "Never. And before you ask, I'm clean, too."

A small smile tugged at her lips. There was something special they could share that was just them. She could feel him, with no barriers, and she could be a first for him in some way. It was a huge frickin' deal to her. So much that she wanted to jump up and down, cheering. This was a step in taking their trust to a deeper level.

"Goodnight," he said.

"Wait, what?" She all but leapt toward the door to stop him. "You're still leaving?"

"Yes."

"Why?"

He took a single step toward her and kissed her hard,

groaning when he pulled away.

"Because I had a purpose for coming here tonight, and sex wasn't it."

He looked her over like he might a fine dessert he wasn't allowed to eat, and then he finally let himself out. She stood in shock. That wasn't the reaction she'd been expecting, and her heart felt a little heavier than normal. Not with rejection, though. With realization. Sebastian has exercised his control. And if his purpose of stopping by hadn't been sex…

"He came to check on me," she whispered to herself. The idea made butterflies dance in her stomach. If it was *just* about sex between them, he would have taken her up on her offer right then, and that's what they would have done.

But he cared. On a deeper level than the physical.

She might have a new mission of keeping Sebastian for longer than their two weeks, but in the meantime, she had a feeling her emotions were going to be a torn to shreds trying to figure this guy out.

Whatever walls he'd put up, they were thicker and higher than she'd thought.

• • •

Sebastian couldn't get his body to stop pounding like a damn drum. As he drove down the dark road, away from Penny and toward his home, all he could think about was how she'd feel with nothing between them.

That was a lot of power to give a woman.

But to be with her?

No holds barred. No barrier. Nothing but them and passion and opportunity.

He turned down the dirt road that led to his property on the outskirts of town. He did like his privacy. Especially lately, when those private moments were spent with Penny. But the idea of being inside her anywhere, anytime?

That was a heady notion.

It was also a tricky one. He prided himself on being good at reading women. Penny was a firecracker. Pushed his buttons. But tonight, she'd been upset and tried to play it off like another challenge. But he'd seen it. The glimpse of hurt in her eyes at the idea he had a date with someone else.

This wasn't just a good time anymore. At some point, it had become something much more. His nightmare scenario, the one he stuck to the two week arrangement to avoid, had happened barely a week in.

What was he supposed to do? End their arrangement early? She was already getting attached. And Christ, he wasn't doing a great job of not getting sucked in either.

Maybe he could urge her to find a date for the rehearsal. Yes, technically that was supposed to be their last day and night together. He wanted that last night.

But what if they showed up with other people? Then they'd both have a clear understanding that this arrangement between them was ending. Yes, it was either that or end it now.

But the thought of giving her up early? He'd never have this chance again. So he had a new mission: keep Penny for the rest of their time together while putting distance between them...

Sounds easy enough.

Yeah fucking right.

Chapter Nine

Penny dropped off food at table seven, trying not to look over at the occupied booth where Sebastian, Huck, Colt, and Ryder sat.

Ever since last night, she'd been wracking her brain about Sebastian and their predicament. If she were to convince him—without pushing him so hard he ran away—that they could make their relationship work past the two week mark, she'd need a plan. One she hadn't quite fine-tuned yet.

But it had been damn near twenty-four hours since he'd stood in her kitchen and she'd confessed yet another embarrassing aspect of her life. She didn't want him to think she was weak. Now, he and the Diamond Rat Pack sat in her restaurant, waiting on their dinner, while she pretended to be thinking of something other than Sebastian's mouth. More specifically, how it felt on her body.

"Order up," cook said when the barbecue ribs were ready.

She grabbed the plates and made the long trek over to the booth. Her only plan of action was to take a step back and observe. If she got a better read on Bass, really saw what was going on beneath this surface façade he kept, maybe she could crack it better.

This was the time for her inner MacGyver to shine—sneakily disassembling one man's commitment-phobia.

His past was working against him. How he'd been raised and the fact that his mother had left weren't secrets. They'd shaped how he viewed relationships. If she could show him she truly cared, show him that she'd never break his trust, maybe there was hope.

Though she didn't have much to compare it to, she felt his struggle, his feelings. It was in the way he touched her face. The way his eyes lingered. The way he gave her everything when she begged, screamed, and whispered. He wanted her to feel like a complete woman. And she wanted to make him feel like a complete man.

"Have you been avoiding me?" Ryder said as she set down the guys' food.

"Of course not." She smiled at her big brother. "I've been avoiding all of you." They turned their heads in question. "I'm kidding," she said. "Calm down."

"Speaking of people you may want to avoid," Colt said, adjusting in his seat. "Here comes one now."

There was a guilty look on Colt's face, then she heard Jenna's voice ring out from behind her.

"Hello," she said happily.

She turned to find her friend in exercise clothes with a yoga mat strapped to her back and…oh shit. Finn was walking in with her.

The physical therapist was in exercise clothes too. She guessed they were coming from Jenna's Yoga in the Park evening class.

Finn smiled. "Good to see you again, Penny."

"How are you?"

"Great."

"You'll never believe this," Jenna said, "but I was talking to Finn, and he said that he doesn't have a date for the rehearsal, Colt."

Penny glared at Colt, and he palmed his baseball cap. The man used to stare down bulls for a living, but he was squirming in his seat.

"Fancy that," Colt said.

This whole thing smelled of a setup, and she was on the chopping block.

• • •

You've got to be fucking kidding me.

Bass almost let the words slip out, but luckily he caught himself. Penny was getting set up, something she wasn't taking too kindly to, and frankly, neither was he.

"Do you want to sit?" Huck asked, oblivious.

"I was going to grab a quick drink at the bar," Finn said, eyeing Penny in a way that made Sebastian's blood heat. He wasn't staring down her tits or anything, but he definitely glanced at them for a much longer moment than he liked.

"Well, I was just headed back that way," she said, and Finn followed her. Like a damn puppy. Which he was. Granted, her ass did invoke men to follow, so he couldn't blame the guy.

But still.

"What the hell?" Bass asked Colt. "You really are playing matchmaker now, huh?"

"No," Colt said as his soon-to-be wife slid next to him. He kissed Jenna's cheek. "This devilish one here is."

"Look, Penny needs to get out there. She doesn't have a date for the rehearsal, and without one, I'm afraid she's going to spend most of the night in the kitchen. I thought Finn would be perfect. He's single, has a great job, and he's cute."

"Cute?" Colt said, frowning.

Jenna smiled and rubbed his leg under the table. At least, he hoped it was his leg. One look from her and Colt's whole expression changed. She whispered something in his ear, and judging by the look on his buddy's face, it put him at ease.

Those two were so lovey it gave Sebastian the dry heaves. Surely someone at this table would be on his side.

He turned his focus to Ryder. "You think this is a good idea? Whatever happened to you going ape shit on anyone who looked at your sister?"

Ryder shrugged. "Finn took her out a while back. He's been respectable in trying to get her attention, and he's solid. Besides, the rehearsal dinner will be loaded with people, and Finn's not *that* type of guy." Ryder glanced at the bar, and so did Bass. Finn was chatting Penny up, and the heat in Bass doubled. When he'd come in the other week to talk to Penny, he'd noticed Finn talking to her. But this time was different. Because a lot had happened in the short time he'd spent with her.

"What does that mean?" Bass asked. "That type of guy? Finn's still a guy."

Ryder took a swig of his drink. "He's not a real threat."

"Not a real threat?" he snapped. Didn't anyone care that she was getting hooked up with…with…

A guy that's perfect for her.

"Look at him, man," Ryder said. "He's her type. Loyal, responsible—"

"How the hell would you know her type? You're her brother. You don't know what she's like—" Bass stopped himself, because his best friend was looking at him like he'd lost his damn mind. Maybe he had.

Hadn't he just thought to himself that Penny needed a date for the wedding? It would put both of them in the right mind. Remind them that what they had was temporary. But seeing the safe, respectable choice of a man that Ryder approved of for the sweet girl next door was too much to take.

Because that made it more clear than ever that he was not *that type* of guy.

AKA: Not Penny's type. No matter how much that truth stabbed his gut, he would be wise to follow through with his plan and push her away. Rather, push her toward someone else. If they both had a date for the rehearsal, that would be golden confirmation that their two weeks were done.

"What is your problem?" Ryder said. "Finn practically walks around with a boy scout badge on. He's not the cheating kind. He doesn't abandon women. He's long term, and that's what Penny deserves. I'm not trying to make my sister a celibate misery case. I just want her to find what she's looking for."

"And you think that's Finn?"

"I think he's as close as it gets."

Bass took another look at the tall, lean man. He was generic, safe, and steady. Likely wanted the same things Penny did. A commitment, house, and kids. The guy would probably run his future son's little league team someday.

Another jab of pain sliced through his stomach. Finn *was* perfect for her. But Penny Diamond went beyond generic. She was incredible. He knew this first hand, but he couldn't do a damn thing about it.

So he sat there, fuming at the fact that he wasn't good enough for her. A fact he'd always known but never had to stare down until that moment.

If anything, he was standing in the way of what she wanted. It would be selfish of him to keep her from the long-term happiness she deserved.

Two weeks was all he had with her. That was it. Then they were friends.

No reason to make her miss out now.

When she walked back to the table, her smile turned to a frown. She leaned in close to Jenna and in a harsh whisper said, "What are you doing?"

"Looks like she's setting you up," Huck said, taking a bite of his burger.

"No kidding. But I told you I don't need a date for the rehearsal."

Jenna's eyes went wide. "So he asked you?"

"Yes, he did. What am I supposed to say?"

"You're supposed to say yes," Sebastian said, and her green eyes shot to him.

"Excuse me?"

"You heard me, darlin'."

"You want me to say yes to Finn for a date?"

He swallowed hard and kept his mouth shut just long enough for Ryder to give his two cents. Which he did.

"He seems like a nice guy," Ryder said.

"Well, thanks for your input, brother, but—"

"Finn *is* your type," Bass said. "You should take him up on his offer. Never know, could be the start of something real."

She looked as though she'd just been slapped, and Bass felt like he'd just been shanked in the gut. Those green eyes looked at him with such pain.

Before he could take back what he'd said, she closed her eyes and shook her head.

"I've got to get back to work." With that, she walked away.

Jenna sighed. "I was just trying to help."

Colt rubbed her back. "I know, sugar."

"Why can't things just work? Penny's great, and I want her to have fun. She deserves some fun."

Bass took a deep breath. She deserved a hell of a lot more than that.

· · ·

It had been a long night, and after politely postponing her decision about Finn's offer—he'd ask her again sooner than later—she'd also had to pretend that Bass hadn't just ripped her heart out of her chest. He might already be intent on replacing her, but she hadn't given up hope yet. At the very least, she wanted an explanation.

She sped down the dirt road that led to his home. It was late, but she wanted to get this cleared up. When she pulled closer, there were a few outdoor lights on, and Sebastian was shooting hoops in the driveway.

She parked, got out of her car, and slammed the door shut.

"What the hell!" she yelled.

He didn't stop shooting. He was breathing hard, sweating, shirtless, and holy shit, it made her forget what she'd come to yell about.

"It's a little late, thought you'd be tired after your long shift and date planning." He did a layup.

"You're the one who pushed me to accept Finn's offer."

He glanced at her, then took another shot, missing, the ball ricocheting toward her. She caught it and held on to it, forcing him to face her.

"Yeah, so?" he said, placing his hands on his hips. His low slung shorts showed off his rock hard abs and narrow hips, and she squeezed the ball tighter to keep from reaching out to touch him.

"So, you want me with another man? Whatever happened to 'when we're together the woman is mine'?" she said in an exaggeratedly low voice, mimicking his words to her.

"Yeah, that's true. But the rehearsal is the last night of our arrangement. No sense in saying no to the perfect guy."

"Perfect guy? Is that what you think I want? Someone like Finn?"

"He's a long term kind of man," he said.

She was getting so fired up she was ready to throw the ball at the stubborn attorney.

"Funny to hear you say *long term* like it's a disease. You know, you're the one that showed up at my place the other night."

"I'm also the one who left," he grated.

"You're *also* the one who came to 'check on me' last night. That had nothing to do with sex."

He paused a minute, and she couldn't help but smile.

"Uh-oh, does the big bad attorney have feelings he's not sure how to deal with?"

"We're still friends."

"That's it? There's nothing else you feel for me?" she asked, but not entirely sure she wanted the answer.

He laughed and looked at the sky. "What do you want me to say? Obviously I'm attracted to you."

She nodded. "But just for two weeks, right? Then you'll magically stop being attracted to me? I start dating Finn, you have some backup woman waiting for you, and we all go on our merry way. Is that how you see this playing out?"

"Yes," he growled.

She bounced the ball once. "Okay. So it doesn't bother you to think about me with Finn. Kissing him." Bounced the ball again. "Touching him."

"Stop it." He looked ready to spit nails. "You say this shit to get a rise out of me."

"I'm trying to get the truth out of you."

He stood still, not moving, not speaking. She was ready to either burst into tears or scream. She was fighting for the right to his heart. And he was a tough competitor.

But if she gave up on him, she'd only fulfill what he thought to be true. Until he told her, showed her, he didn't want her, she'd hang on to him.

"What about a compromise?" she said.

His ears perked. "Depends what you mean by compromise."

She took a deep breath, prepping herself for the risk she was about to take.

"Everyone is so set on us having dates to the rehearsal.

Why don't *we* go together?"

His dark eyes sparkled with confusion. "For several reasons. One is that we're keeping our relationship from everyone. Showing up together would be a big fucking declaration, the opposite of discretion."

Okay, so he wasn't one for big declarations, she'd figured that. "It doesn't have to be this big deal," she said. "We can show up together as friend-ish type things. That's not a crazy notion."

"Did you just say friend-ish type things?"

She glared.

He shook his head. "Whatever it is, it's still a statement. One that your brother and everyone else will figure out. Then we'll have to explain why we're not together the next day."

"Of course, because God forbid we go beyond two weeks."

His expression seemed pained. "You agreed to the terms," he said. "Why are you trying to change them now?"

"Because I want you!" And she wanted him for a lot longer than fourteen days. But she felt like she was on the brink of losing him already, and it had nothing to do with the timeline.

He ran a hand through his hair, and it looked like he was trying to fight off his brain from exploding. But she went on. Pushed. Because she had to know if she was fighting a losing battle. "The question is, do you want me back?"

Those dark eyes zeroed in on her. "Yes." He sounded pissed off by his own admission. "But that doesn't change our arrangement. Showing up at the rehearsal dinner, making a statement like that gets us nowhere. It actually puts us in a worse position. Because the next day, we're done."

That struck her chest like a dull knife to the ribs. "Did

you ever decide about Jenna's friend? Are going to the wedding with the third bridesmaid?"

He nodded. "I told Colt I'd show her around. She'll be here for a couple of weeks while he and Jenna are gone."

"Ah yes, and a couple of weeks is your specialty," she snapped.

"Don't." He took a step closer. "Don't act like you aren't doing the same thing."

"You're the one who pushed me toward Finn. I haven't said yes to him yet."

He scoffed, and all the hard muscles of his chest and abs flexed. "I'm not talking about just that. Don't pretend that you're innocent in all of this. *You* sought *me* out, remember? *You're* the one who agreed to the two weeks, because you're on a mission to gain experience and find a better man when we're done."

A left hook to the kidney would have packed less of a punch. Because he was right. She had set this up, agreed, with the end goal that she'd walk away with sexual experiences, know herself as a woman better, and find the kind of man she wanted long term.

But how could she have guessed Bass would turn out to be that man?

"You made it clear that when we're together, it's us," she said. "The woman is yours, remember? I'm that woman right now. Until the two weeks is up."

"Or until you say no," he said.

She nodded. "Well I haven't said no, and the rehearsal dinner is on my time." And she would fight for her time. "So, we'll try this another way," she said, then shot the ball, swishing it.

He looked at her with shock.

"I played in high school," she said, shrugging. "I may not have as much experience as you, but I can hold my own."

Judging by the glare on his face, he knew she wasn't talking just about basketball anymore.

"I want to finish out the week with you because I like spending time with you. More than anyone I've ever been with," he admitted.

"Do you care about me?" she asked.

After a moment, he said, "Of course I do."

"More than friendship?"

He clenched his teeth.

"You promised me the truth," she said. "Said this whole thing is built on trust."

He took a deep breath. He was obviously racing to think of a clever way to speak his way out of this one. But she wasn't having it.

"I asked you a question," she said, using words he'd used on her. That got his attention in a hurry.

He stalked toward her with a lust-crazed look. "What I feel for you goes so far beyond friendship it's fucking laughable."

That made her stall. So there was hope.

"However—" he started, but she cut him off. She was clinging to that hope. And the best way to bring the real Sebastian out, was a challenge.

"So here's the deal." She dribbled the ball, walking toward him. "First one to make a basket wins."

She nudged his sweaty chest as she passed him, gingerly making her way toward the hoop.

"What are your terms?" he asked.

"If I win, you take me to the rehearsal dinner. As my

date. And we'll deal with the aftermath later."

"Penelope…" he warned.

But she didn't care. This was her shot. Literally. "Deal?"

"And what if I win?"

She looked at him. "What would you like?"

He growled and moved in front of her. His hard chest was now a wall between her and the basket.

"If I win, I'm going to tie you up and spank your ass for pulling this stunt. Then I'm going to fuck you until sunrise." He leaned in and bit her earlobe. "And if you beg me long enough, I may just let you come too."

She licked her lips. "Sounds like a win-win to me." Her words stuttered a little, because the look on his face was not only serious, it was brutal.

Being on the brink of pleasure with him all night, only for him to deny her over and over, did sound like a special kind of torture.

"Deal," she said, pushing his chest with her shoulder and making him step back. It was a single second, but it gave a clear shot, and she took it.

But the ball hit the back board, swirled around the hoop, and fell out and onto the ground. Bass was there to rebound and toss it back up, sinking the basket for himself.

Her mouth dropped, half in shock, half in excitement, because he tossed the ball aside and headed straight toward her. She should be disappointed she'd lost, but if there was ever a chance to show him he could trust her and make this work, now was it.

"You're in trouble now, darlin.'" Not stopping until he reached her, he tangled his fingers through her hair and kissed her hard.

She groaned at the contact and wrapped her arms around him. He kissed her like a wild man. Biting and sinking his tongue deep. Their teeth clattered, tongues dueled, and she clung to his bare back, sinking her nails in. Anything to get him closer.

Without breaking the hot kiss, he hoisted her up, and she wrapped her legs around his hips as he carried her toward the house.

"You fuck with my mind...make me crazed," he said, biting down her neck.

She drove both hands into his hair and moaned, giving him all the access to her she could. Her skirt was riding up, and her boots were digging into his ass, causing his shorts to slink even lower.

She eased her hold on him just long enough to pull her tank top over her head, then she was back to hugging him. He kissed and bit the top of her cleavage, then bit her nipple through the lacy cup of her bra.

"Ah!" It stung but felt so good. She couldn't slow down, couldn't let him slow down, even if she wanted to. She wanted all of him. All the passion, heat, and raw ferocity that was Sebastian Strafford.

"Can't wait," he growled. Her bare back hit the cold front door. "I warned you," he said, propping her against the door while he used one hand to shove his shorts down, then tear her panties off.

He was strong. His muscles flexed to keep her up while he brought the same free hand to her mouth.

"Suck," he said harshly.

She did. She sucked all four of his fingers as deeply as she could. But as soon as he buried them in her mouth, he retreated, then reached between their bodies and used his newly moist fingers to coat his hard cock.

In one hard thrust, he buried himself inside her.

He stilled. His dark eyes wide with equal parts awe and shock. He stared at her with so much amazement he looked on the brink of pain.

"I feel you," he said, moving his hips subtly, as if reveling in the feel of their connection without any barriers. She knew this was the first time he'd ever felt a woman with no condom, and her chest wanted to burst with pride and happiness that she was the one giving this to him. That this was something special that they would always share.

He closed his eyes for a moment and rested his forehead against hers, thrusting once so deeply, so powerfully that she cried his name.

"More," he groaned. "I need more." Gripping her ass, he took just that. Fucking her hard. The cold door against her back, banging wildly with every punishing thrust.

"Penny," he groaned, thrusting hard, then stirred deep, "Never like this. You feel incredible."

"So do you." With her fingers tunneled through his hair and her heels clamped around his back, she kissed him hard. He swallowed every moan and sigh.

She bit his lip. "I want all of you."

And he gave it. Surging deep, so hard and consuming and intense that she felt his energy transfer to her like a shot of adrenaline. Powerful and raw.

"Yes, yes, like that. All of it," she said.

He'd told her once to give it all up to him. Now it was her turn to demand the same. She peppered kisses along his temple, his cheek, the corner of his mouth.

"I'm going to come," he said.

"Yes."

"I want to come in you. So fucking much."

"Yes," she said again, shifting her hips to take him deeper, her ass continuing to bang against the door.

"What have you done to me?" he said around a strangled breath, and she felt his strong body tense. His release was so intense, so hot and powerful that it sent her spiraling over the edge and into her own climax.

She cried his name, and after a few moments of being clamped around him, he opened the door, keeping her right where she was, his cock still inside her, and walked into the room.

She bobbed on top of him as he kicked the door shut and headed toward the bedroom. Her eyes went wide when she realized he was still hard.

"I told you, darlin'," he rasped, then bit her neck. "You're in trouble. And we're nowhere near done."

. . .

Sebastian's world: Just. Fucking. Changed. And he had a feeling he wouldn't know how to deal with that until tomorrow. Because right then, all he could think about was how it felt to come inside Penny.

She was still wrapped around him as he entered the bedroom. He tossed her on the bed, hating the warmth he gave up, but loving the way her breasts bounced damn near out of her bra.

"Strip," he said, barely recognizing his own voice. "I want you naked. Now." He did the same, removing the few pieces of clothing left. When they were both naked, he said, "Get on your hands and knees and raise your ass in the air."

Her body gently trembled. She'd gotten off, and he'd wanted to make her earn it. But he'd been lost. Between her mouth, her pussy, and being so deep in such a hot wet paradise, he could barely think.

He was hard and ready to feel her again. Christ, he was starting to worry he'd never get enough.

She positioned herself like he'd said, but she was in the middle of the bed, and he stood at the foot of it. Too far. She was too far away, and space was the last thing he wanted. He gripped her heels and tugged her to the edge.

She yipped in surprise but readjusted to her knees, and with that perfect ass in the air, she looked over her shoulder at him.

"You going to punish me now?"

"You like it when I do?"

She swayed her ass left to right and smiled. "Yes."

Jesus, his perfect woman had come to life and was right there, on his bed, ripe for the taking. Everything about her screamed innocent and naïve. Maybe part of her was. But she was a tough woman with desires that seemed to rival his own. All this time, Sebastian had looked the part of the hedonist. Who knew that Miss Diamond played it?

He palmed her ass hard, and she threw her head back, all that red hair splaying over her back. It was so silky and shiny that he couldn't help but reach out and run one hand over it and down her spine.

It was like petting his own personal kitten. She was his.

He was about to tell himself no, remind himself this was a short lived arrangement, when something caught him off guard.

Her green eyes flashed at him. "I can still feel you," she whispered. And arched against his touch. "I feel you all the time. After you leave is the worst part. But this time?" She pushed back a little, causing him to grip her ass tighter. "I *really* feel you."

He looked at her beautiful skin, bright eyes, and vibrant hair. She was gorgeous. Her round ass was perfect and waiting to be pinkened by his hand. Oh, this woman deserved a spanking. And he'd give it. Based on last time, she'd get wet from it. Hell, the woman was already soaking.

"Jesus," he rasped as he looked between her legs. She had the prettiest pussy he'd ever seen.

An animalistic urge to fuck her again and again, to never let her leave his bed, was overwhelming. He'd never been so close to a woman before. Never trusted anyone to the extent he trusted her. Never seen his fate flash before his eyes until this moment.

At some point, he'd gotten away from himself and given in to her.

And he couldn't be upset about it. Not then.

He did everything he could to sear this moment into his brain. Her tousled hair, glossy eyes, and smile. She looked well-loved. By him.

He'd deal with all the reasons he was digging himself into a hole. But not today.

Tomorrow.

Now, he needed her. Wanted her. Was consumed by the need to keep her. Just for the night. For the week. Didn't matter. He'd take tonight. Because for now, she was his alone. Not Finn's, not some nameless, faceless man who could give her a future she wanted. Not the man from her past who'd broken her heart.

She was *his*. Simply. And he'd take advantage while he could.

"I'm going to feel you first," he said, running his finger along her damp slit.

"Yes, anything you want." She pushed back, trying to coax his finger inside, and he couldn't deny her. Sliding in, he felt her hot, tight sheath grip him. Only this time, she was soaking from him. He'd coated her. Brought her to climax. Remained a part of her.

The idea was drugging, and he couldn't get enough.

"You had a plan from the beginning," he said, thrusting deeper. "You had a…what was it? Mission?" He curved his finger.

"Y-yes."

"And you wanted me. Put me in this position to take you. And you beg for more, even now."

"Yes," she said, the words coming out a moan.

"You're not the good girl everyone thinks you are."

"Yes, I am," she said, her heavy eyes looking over at him again. "I'm only a bad girl with you."

He liked the sound of that, so he rewarded her with another finger.

"Oh, God…" She sighed, and her body tensed.

"Not going to come already are you?" he teased.

"I want to."

"I know you do, but you already broke the rules and came once before I said you could."

"Because you were fucking me, and I loved it—"

His fingers surged into her, and she gasped. "I still told

you not to. Told you I'd punish you."

"Yes, please do it. Anything," she groaned. Yeah, she was close.

Between the feel of her tightening around him and his cock twitching with the need to be back in wet paradise, he removed his fingers and plunged his cock deep.

"Penny…"

Her name was the only thing he could say. His control was slipping, and all he wanted to do was bring her pleasure. Wanted to stay right there, buried deep in her heat. He could feel how wet he'd left her.

He slid in and out, the motion of his hips slamming against her ass, and it wasn't enough.

He wrapped one arm around her waist and yanked her back.

"Oh God! You're so deep." And with the added moisture, he slid with ease, allowing him to go further than ever before.

His arm around her waist tightened as he took her hard and slow.

She collapsed from her hands to her elbows, and Bass took full advantage.

Keeping a hold on her, he pulled out all the way and delivered a slap on her ass, rocking her forward and making her groan.

"Do you know why I'm punishing you?"

"B-because I challenged you."

He thrust hard inside once, then slapped her ass again, causing her to fist the sheets.

"No. Don't you ever," thrust, "think I don't want you." His mind was a haze, and the words were out before he could get a grip on what he was saying or feeling. "Do you understand me?" he growled. "I told you, you're mine." For however long that lasted. Until their relationship was over, she was his. Completely.

He slapped her ass again and took her with all his might.

"Say it, Penny!"

"Yes. Yes, I understand."

"Good girl." He kept up his penetrating pace, and she started heaving, trying not to come. Despite what he'd said, he didn't want her unsatisfied. If things were different, his goal in life would be to keep her happy.

Where did that *come from?*

He pushed the thought aside.

"Come now, darlin'," he whispered.

He felt her tight pussy instantly, milking him from her release. "Thank you," she said in such a sweet, trusting tone. The words hit his chest like a shot. She'd denied herself to make him happy. Held out. For him.

Between the surge of pleasure that raced through his spine and the tug of emotion that shot through his chest, he couldn't take it anymore.

This woman amazed him.

He was lucky to have her, even for a short time.

Penelope Diamond is way out of my league.

As his own climax hit, he imprinted every inch of her to memory. For however long he had her, he would cherish her.

Soon, they'd go back to friends. The thought made him sick. So he stirred, feeling her arch to his touch.

But not tonight.

Tonight they weren't friends, and he heard her sweet mouth admit, understand, she was his.

Tonight, she was his.

Chapter Ten

"I can't believe you're getting married so soon!" Lily said to Jenna as Penny set out a towel on the banks of Diamond Lake.

"I know! I'm so excited."

The girls set up next to Penny, with Lily's son Alex playing beside them. The lake was already packed with most of the town's population lining the lake banks around the large lake. Lounge by the Lake Day was a tradition for the last Saturday in May. A pre-party to kick off summer.

Two days had passed since she and Sebastian had enjoyed their little fight-makeup sex session. She didn't know what to make of it. Other than to wonder if he was pulling away. She didn't want to push him too hard too fast, but what they'd shared went beyond friendship and their arrangement. They both knew it. So why did she feel that every time they took one step toward real intimacy, he was one step closer to running the other direction?

"There's Colt!" Jenna said, and she took off running in the direction of the guys walking toward them. Huck, Ryder, and Colt, who was carrying a cooler, were several yards away. No Sebastian.

"You okay?" Lily said.

Penny turned to face her friend. "I don't know."

Lily looked her over, then turned to her son. "Alex, honey." She tugged on the boy's life jacket, making sure it was secure. "Want to go play with Michael? He's right there with his mom." Lily pointed to where they were at the edge of the lake.

Michael's mom was waving him over. Lily waved, and the moms exchanged some signal that apparently meant Michael's mom would keep an eye on the boys for a few minutes.

Lily's attention turned to Penny. "What's going on?"

Penny shrugged. She needed to talk to someone, get some perspective, but she couldn't go around talking about her and Sebastian.

"I'm thinking about a lot, about the future."

Lily nodded. "Does this thinking involve another person?"

"Sort of." How could she talk about this without revealing everything? Vagueness would have to be her friend. "I want certain things. Like a family, husband, and all that."

Lily nodded.

"But it's more than that. I have this picture in my head of making biscuits in the morning, then having coffee with my husband while sitting on the porch and watching the sunrise."

"You want a home."

"Yeah," Penny said.

That was it exactly. And more than that. She wanted Sebastian. Because being in his arms, his warm breath against her neck, felt like home.

She shook her head. She'd known better than to go into details about what her brain churned out, but with summer gearing up, she couldn't help but think of her mother. It was the one season Penny missed her the most, because it was the one time of year they'd had all their adventures together. Along with all the wedding and love bliss in the air, she couldn't help but confide in her friend.

"I have this image of my husband setting up a swing set in the front yard. My dad coming home for Christmas and…" *And not avoiding me like he has since mom died.*

Penny knew that was why her father didn't come around or talk to her much. She wouldn't make him admit it, but she knew it was because she looked just like her mother. With her passing, and then Penny taking over the BBQ, her father couldn't handle the reminder, so he'd bought a condo in Florida. She spoke to him a few times a year. They used to be close, but it was like the sight of her, the sound of her voice, made him cringe.

Which broke her heart, because her father and mother had had a marriage that she envied. They'd shown her what real love looked like. While she didn't doubt her father loved her, she knew he was grieving, a process Penny still hadn't figured out how to get through. She couldn't shake the feeling that the people she loved might at any time disappear, the same way her mother had.

"It's wonderful to want all those things," Lily said. "And you'll have them."

"I want other things too. Like passion."

"Ah." Lily nodded. "And you think you can't have both?"

She knew she couldn't. Because Bass was passion and heat and every naughty fantasy she'd wrapped up into a big ball of lawyer awesomeness. But the rest? Like a future or commitment or house? No, he had made it clear a long time ago that he didn't do any of those things. She might have to realize that no matter her efforts, he might never want the things she did.

"It's not likely," Penny finally admitted. Not unless she moved on from Bass. But the thought of giving him up stung her chest. She wanted to try. Try for more with him. Try for longer. Try for anything he'd give her.

They'd made strides as a couple, but she knew she was losing him. If she could sell the idea that longer term wasn't scary, maybe he'd push the two week end date back.

Maybe. That was a far cry from yes.

But *maybe* was a lot better than no. It was a delicate situation, and she had to approach it as such. Not her strong point. Since every time Bass came around, her bratty, challenging side came out, which recently had ended with her begging or screaming his name.

"I'm not the perfect person to give advice," Lily said, glancing at Alex playing by the water. "But you have to decide what you're willing to give up and what you're willing to fight for." She patted Penny's shoulder. "If there's something or someone you want, make it happen. But don't chase a dream that isn't there. Sometimes, you have to adjust your expectations."

She nodded. Lily was right. Problem was, she didn't know which expectation to adjust. If it came to her prince charming or fairy tale ending, which one would she choose if they didn't match up? She looked over Lily's shoulder and saw Sebastian walking toward them.

He'd come.

Shirtless, in board shorts and aviator glasses, a towel slung over one shoulder, and all that tan skin. When he smiled her direction, her heart fluttered.

He was what she wanted her happily ever after to look like.

Before she could drool and swoon her fill, a different voice came from behind her.

"Penny?"

She turned, recognizing the voice enough to make bile rise in her throat.

"Eli."

He stood next to his fiancée, a tall platinum blonde in a skimpy bikini. With abs like hers, her number one hobby was obviously Cross Fit.

She'd thought seeing Eli again would be weird, but he didn't look the least bit awkward. In fact, he looked smug. As if purposefully parading his new woman in front of Penny, reminding her how she was lacking.

"You still look adorable as ever," Eli said. "I hear you're running the BBQ now."

"That's right," she said tightly.

Lily looked between her and Eli. Penny just put on her best smile. She wasn't the same woman he'd dumped. She was stronger, more confident.

"Maybe we should stop in sometime," he said, squeezing platinum's side. "Cindy here's a vegetarian though. May be difficult to find something for her."

Heat engulfed Penny. And not the good kind. The kind

that made her want to run and hide. All she could think about
was how small she felt. How Eli was loving this, and Penny
was letting this happen. There was no graceful way out.

"You should call for a reservation first," Sebastian said,
walking up behind her, cupping her waist, and pulling her
into his side. His voice was full of pride and made her tingle.
"The BBQ fills up pretty quick."

She looked up at Sebastian with a questioning expression. He just smiled down at her, then returned his attention
to Eli.

"Really?" Eli said. "It never got that crowded in the past."

"Well, that was the past. Penny has a way of—" Bass looked
at her and briefly ran his hand from the small of her back to
her ass and back up "—making things hot and addicting."

That made Eli pause, and Lily looked like she was barely stifling a smile. Then platinum actually checked out Sebastian, and that was Penny's final straw.

"Well, I can't say it was good running in to you," she said.
"But have a nice day."

She turned away from him, and Bass was right there
giving her the support she needed.

Eli mumbled something, grabbed Platinum, and walked
off. Maybe Penny was finally turning into the woman she
always wanted to be. And looking up at the handsome man
that came to her rescue but let her fight for her own victory,
she couldn't help but smile.

• • •

Jesus, Penny was gorgeous. Especially when she looked up at
him with that smile. It actually made his chest hurt.

He'd seen Eli approach her. The asshole had actually gone out of his way to make his presence known. But she had stood tall.

"That was sweet, Bass," Lily said.

He frowned. "What was?"

"You know, pretending to be with Penny to piss Eli off. I almost believed it for a second."

He cleared his throat, reminding himself that they weren't alone.

Keep it casual.

While the rest of their friends were several yards away, tied up in conversations with other people, Bass was drawn to Penny.

"I'd be the lucky one to have such a lady on my arm." He looked at Penny. Her long hair pulled up, the Kansas sun dancing off her skin. That black bikini top and cut off shorts had his imagination going, but he kept it under control. Lily was standing right there. And besides, he couldn't walk around with a damn hard-on all day.

The woman drives me crazy…

"Well, I'm glad you made it," Lily said, then looked over by the lake. "Ah, crap."

Bass caught sight of what she was looking at: Alex, trying to perfect his cannon ball.

"I'll be back," she said and took off in Alex's direction.

Which left him alone with Penny.

"Can I set up next to you?"

She smiled and took the towel off his shoulder. "I'd like that." She laid it out, and they sat side by side, looking out at the lake like the best of friends without a care in the world. Only he did care…more than he was prepared for.

She lay back, reclining on her forearms, and he sat with his hands tangled together and draped over his bent knees. They were best kept there.

He glanced around. Jenna and Colt were sneaking kisses and easing into the water. Lily was busy with Alex, and the whole town of Diamonds seemed to be having a great time.

He wouldn't mind stealing a kiss of his own from the pretty redhead with a wicked mouth. But he couldn't. A fact he hated.

"How are you?" he asked. Small talk wasn't his style, but he didn't know what else to say.

She looked at him and smiled. "Better now. Wishing I could touch you."

That took him by surprise. Then again, she wasn't shy when it came to what she wanted.

All he could do was smile and be just as honest. "Me too, darlin'."

"Oh?" She sat up a little. "Where would you like me to touch? If we could, right now, that is."

"Everywhere," he answered instantly, like some damn teenager on the brink of getting to second base if he said all the right things.

"Okay then." She fished for something out of her little bag. "Sit just like you are and keep your eyes forward."

Just when he was going to ask what she was doing, much less why she was ordering him around, he saw a tub of sunscreen in her hand, and she moved behind him.

"You're getting a little hot," she said in his ear from behind him. "I can help with that."

The cold feeling of sunscreen squirting onto his back almost made him jump. It was pathetic how easily she made him edgy.

But when her hands started spreading the lotion around his shoulders, down his spine, and then back up, he almost groaned at the sensation. Her small thumbs dug into his muscles, kneading as she massaged him.

He stayed just as he was, not touching her, hopefully looking completely unaffected. She was just a friend helping him out with sunscreen.

Yeah right.

"I keep thinking about the other night," she whispered.

Shit, that hard-on he was trying to not sport was starting to stir.

"Can't talk about that, darlin'. Unless you want me tenting my shorts all day."

She laughed, and the sound made his whole body flush with a sense of enjoyment and pride. Making her laugh was the best thing he'd done all day.

"Well, then. Why don't we talk about you?"

He glanced over his shoulder with a raised brow. "You know me, not much to talk about."

"So then tell me something I don't know. Like some hidden secret, darkest fear, or fun fact you've hidden from the rest of your world."

There were no fun facts he could think of. Mostly because the parts of himself he kept private weren't fun. They were painful.

"Why do you want to know?"

Her hands stopped for a moment, resting flat on his back. "Because I want to know you more."

There was such a raw honesty in her voice that he couldn't help but respond. She wanted to know him more. She'd said that before. It was still a bad idea, and yet, a big part of him wanted that also. Because he felt the same way. It was an odd idea, but damn it, he wanted it. Despite the two week agreement, they'd always be friends, so even if this ended between them—

When. When this ended. No if.

He had to remind himself that.

And maybe explaining himself would make it easier for her when they had to go back to being friends.

"Bass?" She slid her hands up, a gesture of support, and said the one word that hit his ribs like a damn arrow. "Please."

He took a deep breath. "You want my darkest fear?" he asked. "I'm terrified of losing what I love most. I'm terrified of it ruining me."

He thought he heard her gasp. This wasn't a conversation for a happy day at the lake, or any day for that matter. But this was the first time he'd ever felt the urge to share. The whole truth. Nothing but the truth…

"Why are you scared of losing what you love?"

He swallowed, willing the words to stay down, but instead they came out. "Because I saw what power over another person can do. Saw what humiliation and devastation look like. How one person can turn another inside out and manipulate your life and your future."

"You're talking about your mom and dad?" she whispered.

He nodded.

"That doesn't have to be you. Their situation and how they handled it was their choice. Their failure. I'm sorry you suffered because of it."

"I don't need your pity."

"I'm not pitying you. You're the strongest man I know. I just want you to realize that. You being in someone's life makes *that* person lucky."

He laughed. "Yeah, Penny Diamond is lucky to have me in her life."

"I am," she said. "You've changed me in a way that can't be undone. And I'm happy about that. But even before our arrangement, you were a constant in my life. You've been loyal and kind. I trust you."

Her words hit him hard. She thought he was strong? Thought he was better than what he came from? Trusted him? Thought he was good enough to be on her level?

"What is it you love most?" she asked.

He shook his head. "Nothing." He turned to face her. "Love nothing, fear nothing."

Her green eyes seared into his. He saw sadness there. For him? Probably. Maybe he shouldn't have said anything.

"Then what do you have to live for?"

"I still have fun. But what's the point of loving something if you're just going to lose it?" he asked in a low tone, keeping his eyes locked on hers.

Shit, had he said that out loud? He hadn't meant to. But looking at her face, those lips, that concern and sadness in her eyes made all his defenses crumble.

He knew now that not spending every moment with her was the definition of missing out. And he was the poor bastard that was suffering. Which should just prove how badly he needed to cut this off.

Before he could put his face of stone on and spout his reminder of their deal, she squeezed his hand, not seeming to care if anyone noticed.

"Certain things are worth the risk. I hope you realize that you're something incredible."

A brick would have been preferable to what settled in his chest.

"Penny, I—"

"Hey guys!" Finn said, walking up.

Sebastian instantly pulled his hand from hers and sat straighter. She looked at him like he'd just slapped her, but she shook it off and faced Finn.

"Hi." She smiled, shadowing her eyes with her hand to look up at him.

"Nice day, huh?" he said, glancing at Bass, then back at Penny. Bass just nodded. He hadn't realized until right then that Finn Billings was the one guy in town he might dislike the most. Not because he wasn't a good guy. Ryder was right, he was solid. The man volunteered at the old folk's home for God sake's.

So why did he feel threatened? Sure, Finn was in shape, but Bass outweighed and outstood the guy. And it had nothing to do with size or success.

It had to do with Penny and how right a guy Finn was for her.

"Yes, very nice," she agreed.

"Well, I was just talking with your brother and friends," he said to her and pointed toward the lake where, yep, their crew was hanging out. "Would you come join us? Both of you, of course."

"Oh! Um…" She glanced at Bass. She saw the same thing he did. Ryder was yelling at her to come over, and Jenna was waving her arm and beckoning. Seemed all their friends liked this idea.

"I'm going to sit here for a bit," Bass said and looked at Penny. "You go on."

Jenna then yelled for Penny, and it seemed this mission of getting her a date to the rehearsal was turning into shoving her and Finn together. Bass couldn't blame his friends. They didn't know how he felt about her.

Even if they did, there were things he couldn't change. Finn could give Penny everything she wanted. More, he could give her those things for longer than two weeks.

She stared at him a moment.

"Go on," he said again.

"Here." Finn held out his hand to Penny and helped her up.

"I'll be right there," she said.

Once Finn was out of earshot, Bass said, "Maybe it's best to keep a distance."

She looked hurt, stunned, betrayed. And he wanted to instantly call back his words.

She bent, pretending to straighten her towel, and whispered, "I wish it was you I was walking toward...not away from."

And despite what he'd said, part of him wished she would walk toward him. Stay with him. But maybe she knew what he did, that she would eventually have to walk away from him, because she turned from him and did just that. And he had pushed her to do so.

Chapter Eleven

Sebastian hit the steering wheel of his car. Yesterday at the lake, there'd been so many things he should have said to Penny. She thought he was incredible? Would she feel that way knowing he intended on ending this? That he was knowingly shoving her in the direction of another man?

"I'm an asshole."

He had to say it out loud or else he would forget. Forget that for a moment they could steal a piece of time together where they could be a couple. Do normal things, like go to the lake and hold hands, catch a movie, maybe dinner, then he'd take her back to his place and sink inside her until sunrise.

He closed his eyes. That was a fairytale, and he knew better. Maybe he was a bigger masochist than he realized. The punishment and pain of being with her was getting to him.

Finn was the kind of man she wanted. But the way she

looked at him made him think maybe he could be the kind of man she deserved.

His grand plan had been to push her limits and send her running from him. He combed a hand through his hair. He couldn't think about her with someone else without wanting to punch something. But every time he saw Finn talking to her, they looked...right.

Like a normal couple.

And she deserved to spend time with a man who could offer her a future. That wasn't Sebastian. But that didn't stop him from tasting her, needing her.

Which begged the question: what would it take to actually pursue Penny? In the open? With long term intentions?

That would have to start with the truth and end with some kind of open acknowledgment. Not something he'd ever done.

And there was one person who wouldn't take kindly to him setting his sights on the innocent Miss Diamond, especially for a short term romp.

Ryder.

Bass had never flaunted his tastes, but his best friend knew of them. Knew the kind of man he was and the kind of women he'd been involved with. Knew of his short-term status.

He started his car, needing time and space to think this through.

Chapter Twelve

Penny's third shot was kicking in as she pounded on Sebastian's front door. It was late and had been a crappy day, but it was officially midnight, which meant it was the last day of their secret affair. And here in several hours, the rehearsal dinner would start.

This was still her time. She had the whole day left with Sebastian, and she intended on using it. It was her last chance to show him how great they were together. If there was one thing she'd learned these past weeks—and there was a lot— it was that there was no point in being a sex goddess if she ended up with a lukewarm guy she didn't love.

The whole point to this wasn't coming out the other side to find a man that was comparable to stale bathwater. The man she wanted was on the other side of the door she was staring down. And he was beyond hot in every way.

She knocked again, and he opened the door in nothing but his boxer-briefs and a sleepy expression.

"What can I do for you?"

"It's our last twenty-four hours," she said and stepped inside. "And I want all of them."

"Have you been drinking?" he asked, shutting and locking the door.

"Yes. But I know what I want, and I'm going for it. I'm fighting for you." She might have slurred just a little that time. But damn it, she was running out of time.

Watching his brain work through his thoughts tore something in her chest. She'd hoped her coming out and saying how much she wanted him would be what convinced him to make his own declaration, but she could see it in his face now. He was pulling away from her. And she couldn't take it.

She whispered his name, and then she went in for the one thing she needed—him. She didn't wait for his approval. She stepped forward and wrapped her arms around him.

His skin was warm, and she buried her face in his neck. Then, finally, his strong arms hugged her back, and it was the best feeling she'd ever had.

"It's been a long day," she said against his chest, trying to keep the tears at bay.

"I know, darlin'," he said against her hair.

"Don't send me away." All she wanted was to stay, right there in his arms, because for a brief moment, the world, their situation, and everything she'd been fighting seemed so small. She felt safe. Protected. Loved.

He picked her up and carried her to his room. Laying her in his bed, he pulled the covers around them, and her eyes went instantly heavy. It was then she realized that she was reaching out for him for more than just sex. She was reaching out for comfort. Because she trusted him. A fact that made her eyes heavy and sleep take over.

· · ·

He'd asked her to keep her distance, but she'd come anyway. Funny thing, he wasn't totally upset about that. About the idea that someone like her ran toward him.

He'd been staring at the ceiling for hours. He'd known as soon as she'd declared that she was going to fight to keep him that this had to end. Not after the rehearsal. It had to end today.

His goal had been to put distance between them today. Prepare her for when they had to go back to being friends. But knowing this was the last time he'd see her like this, he couldn't send her away. Even if it made him a bigger asshole, he needed these final hours with her.

He closed his eyes and rested his face against her hair. The smell of strawberries engulfed him. He'd reason with her as soon as they woke up in the morning. But just as his eyes slid shut, he felt the smallest rustling of the petite woman in his arms.

"Bass?" she said.

"I'm here," he whispered.

She turned in his arms, her face against his bare chest. They hadn't done anything sexual, and that somehow made her sleeping next to him more intimate.

"My Sebastian," she murmured in a sleep-soaked voice. The feel of her lips moving against his skin made his cock instantly hard and his chest hurt.

My Sebastian?

She was claiming him.

"Penny?" he whispered back quietly, seeing if he could rouse her from sleep. How was he supposed to handle this? All he could think about was everything that made him wrong for her. But when she wiggled a little, he felt her lips open and deliver a kiss on his chest. He groaned, trying to keep his growing erection from causing a problem. But then she did it again, only this time lower.

Murmuring his name, she peppered his skin with those sweet lips, her long hair blanketing his body as she worked her way down his torso.

"Penny?" he quietly called out, hoping she was asleep and might stop if she realized this wasn't a dream.

"Yes?"

Okay, so she was awake.

"Why don't we talk?"

She glanced up at him. All that wild red hair fanned out and green eyes burning with lust.

"Do you want me to stop?"

God no. But he couldn't tell her that. "I just want to establish a few things and—"

"I know," she said, then closed her mouth over his nipple and gently sucked.

That did him in.

He drove his fingers through her hair and moaned. She straddled his hips and sat up to look into his eyes.

"I want to feel you," she said. "No competition, no rules, no *establishing* any conditions. Just us."

He cupped her face and nodded. He wanted to tell her why that was a bad idea. Tell her that emotions were running too deep, but instead, he just looked at her.

She smiled and leaned down, delivering the hottest kiss Bass had ever felt. Lush, soft, and deep. Everything felt intensified and in slow motion.

Her hands ran down his stomach until she reached the band of his boxers and pulled them down. His cock bobbed between her spread legs, and he had missed the part where she wasn't wearing panties beneath her little dress. Now he knew.

She rubbed against him. Her heat, already wet, as if recognizing him and his body, as hers.

Fuck, he liked the thought of that. He'd always focused on keeping things surface, having a woman for a short period of time, but belonging to each other?

No. He couldn't think of that. Not now. He tried to stay still. Take her advances. But finally he couldn't bear it any longer, he had to touch her.

He sat up, cupping her face and kissing her harder, pausing only to lift her dress over her head and toss it away.

Her beautiful skin glowed in the soft moonlight, and he kissed down her neck, tasting every inch, until he reached her ruby nipples.

"So perfect," he rasped. The feel of her skin against his. Her body so close. Her warmth surrounding him. He wrapped his arms around her tight and pulled one pebbled peak into his mouth.

A little gasp escaped her lips. He circled the peak with his tongue, then sucked again before paying the same attention to the other one. She lifted enough and reached between them to position his cock at her entrance. There was no more warning than her sinking down. He shuddered as her tight heat engulfed him.

He could stay there forever.

His grip tightened, and he licked her nipples, her breasts, her skin. Anything he could get his mouth on.

She wove her fingers though his hair and kissed the top of his head as she began to rock back and forth.

On his lap, with him buried deep inside her, she slowly moved, not letting a single inch of him slip from her. He realized that she was showing him how she felt, and without him realizing what she'd started, she'd reversed their dynamic and was now commanding him. And he was lost to her. He'd do whatever, however she wanted.

"You feel so good," he rasped. "You feel like everything."

It didn't make sense, but he couldn't explain it. Not then. She was *his* everything. Everything good he'd never had. Everything he didn't understand. Just everything. Bad idea or not, he let the word slip out and couldn't bring himself to care.

This level of connection, trust, and intimacy was something he'd never experienced.

Don't think of that now...

"Make love to me," she pleaded against his brow. And that's when he realized, that's what they were doing. She was making love to him. Taking him into her body and her heart and holding on tight. And she wanted him back. Wanted him to take over.

With her legs locked around him, he flipped around so that she lay on her back and he was over her, still blessedly locked between those soft thighs.

He didn't say a word. What could he say? Nothing seemed good or powerful enough. So he wrapped her up tighter, hugging her to him. With his arms smashed between her back and the mattress, he thrust between her legs.

She arched, gasping his name. Keeping every inch of skin touching, he surged inside again. Her legs clamped tighter, her little arms trembling from the tight grip she tried to keep him in.

"I'm there…" she whispered.

Looking into her eyes, he kissed her softly and delivered another thrust.

"Yes…" she said. "Come with me…"

If he'd ever had any hope of denying her, he had none now. Going deep, he grit his teeth and a slow, burning release flared through his entire body.

"God, Penny." He stirred his hips, unwilling to give this up yet but knowing he had to.

The last of his release flooded her. He stayed right there, clinging to the one thing he'd always wanted, but knowing that in the morning, he would have to let her go.

Chapter Thirteen

Penny's eyes fluttered open. She was surrounded by Sebastian's sheets and scent, but not the actual man. It was still early, the sun barely showing signs of coming up through the window. With all the preparations for the rehearsal tonight in the city, she had a lot to get done.

Sebastian seemed to have the same idea, because he walked into the bedroom fully dressed and stared at her from the doorway.

"Good morning…again," she said, sitting up and pulling the sheet with her. She was naked, her skin still buzzing from the incredible toll he had taken on her body.

"We should get going."

He was so still, unmoving from the spot in the doorway as if ready to flee at a moment's notice.

"Is something wrong?" She'd thought what they'd shared was a good thing. It left her with a satisfied smile on her face. But he looked the opposite. Upset even.

"I was prepared for last night, or this morning." His voice was thick and precise, like talking to a client.

"I think things turned out well. I know there's a lot going on today, but maybe after the rehearsal you can come over to my place?"

"No."

She clutched the sheet tighter. What was happening? Where was the man that had held her, made her feel safe and complete? Because he wasn't here. The man she was staring down was pressed, clean, and stone.

"I'm calling it," he said quickly.

She frowned. "What does that mean?"

He keep his dark eyes on hers, his fists clenched. Like some internal struggle was warring within that she had no idea how to help with.

"It means that we're done. Our time is up."

"Tomorrow," she whispered. "Our time is up tomorrow. We still have all day today and tonight."

"No." He glanced at her. "I'm breaking it off early. And I'm going with that woman to the rehearsal tonight."

Her heart sped up. "You have a date lined up for tonight? But we just…"

"Fucked," he said.

The word had never sounded so harsh. She had thought it was more than that.

"You can't tell me you didn't feel something like that. Something real."

"You're right," he said. "And that's why I'm ending this early. I should have ended it a long time ago." He shook his head. "I don't know. Maybe we never should have done it at all."

The weight of Kansas was nowhere near as heavy as his presence. She'd never felt more naïve, more discarded, than she did right then.

He looked at her. Standing tall, fully dressed, and perfectly kempt while she sat naked, a total mess, in a ruffled bed. Her entire chest snapped into two, and she'd never felt so vulnerable, so alone.

She could have sworn a flicker of sadness crossed his face, but it was gone too soon for her to be sure. She had to find some kind of dignity. Even if it was faked.

"You said you should have broken this off sooner? Why didn't you?"

He shook his head but didn't speak.

"Because emotions got involved?" she challenged, hoping she sounded angry. "Whose emotions are you referring to?"

"Yours."

She nodded. "Of course. Because I'm the only one in this, aren't I? I'm the only one who feels something. Certainly not you."

"I should have—"

"Don't! Don't you dare tell me what you should have done, and don't do me any favors."

"It was never my goal to hurt you," he whispered. "You want something I can't give."

"Oh, so you're sparing my feelings, are you?" She gritted her teeth. "I don't need your pity." She was using his words against him, but it didn't make her feel any better. "You're a coward," she said. "You know what you want. She's standing right in front of you. But you're too scared to take a chance."

She stood quickly, yanking on her dress and hating that

she likely looked terrible, especially now that the tears were spilling over her lashes.

"Penny—"

"You asked when we started if I was sure I could handle you. You weren't sure I'd last."

She waited for him to say something, but when he only gave her silence, she walked past him and to the bedroom door.

With her hand on the knob, she said, "You were wrong about one thing." She opened the door. "*I* outlasted *you*."

With that, she slammed the door on everything. Sebastian. Their future together. And the stupid idea that they could ever have been more.

Chapter Fourteen

Bass adjusted his tie as he walked into the hotel where Jenna and Colt were holding the rehearsal. Penny's words had vibrated through his mind since she'd left this morning.

Maybe I am a coward.

What he'd said to her was the hardest thing he'd ever done. And she'd called him on it. Only this time, he didn't want to fight. He'd made the right choice cutting ties with her before the attachment got even worse, but everything in his gut told him he was wrong.

A feeling that intensified when he saw her walk in with Finn. She looked beautiful. The only flaw he could find was whose arm she was on.

What the fuck was I thinking?

Seeing her, not being able to touch her, claim her, feel her…

He'd always valued control above all else, but now he needed something—some*one*—more than that…and he'd let her go.

How could he have stood there and pushed her away? Worse, how could he have pushed her into the arms of another man?

He shook his head, trying to get his brain on track with his thinking. He'd made his choice. Now he had to live with it.

"Sebastian," Jenna said, snapping him from his thoughts. "My third bridesmaid just called. She got held up and won't be here until late."

Great. Not that he cared. He wasn't interested in his next fling. Not when he was watching the only woman he wanted walk away on some other man's arm.

"We can't wait for her," Jenna said. "So tomorrow, will you walk her through everything for the wedding?"

"Sure," he said. Jenna smiled and skipped off. Fucking skipped. She was so happy. Colt was practically drooling. And here Sebastian was, for once all too aware of how isolated he felt without anyone by his side.

"I don't know how to say this buddy," Huck said, coming to stand next to him. "But you look scary pissed." He handed him a tall glass of Southern Comfort.

Bass downed it immediately, then swiped Huck's glass and did the same thing.

"Whoa, take it easy," Huck said.

Bass scoffed. "I need another." Because the drinks weren't doing shit to *comfort* him. Thank God the hotel had a bar. He needed all the distraction he could get, because Penny was on the other side of the room, and he could still smell her. Strawberries.

He didn't know how long he stood there, just staring and realizing she wasn't looking at him. She hadn't even glanced at him as she came into the room.

"Here you go. Maybe go a little slower this time," Huck said, handing him another drink. The man moved quick with alcohol, and Bass appreciated it.

He took another swig, then looked at the glass. He'd lost count of how many swallows he was on. His new goal was to drink until he could forget. Until he couldn't smell or feel her anymore.

"I can still. Fucking. Smell her," he growled. Strawberries and sun and warmth.

"Okay," Huck said, standing next to him. "All I can smell is liquor."

Sebastian tried to smile but failed. "What do you want?"

"I want to know if you're okay. You've been different—"

"*My date* isn't going to make it tonight, it would seem." He raised his glass. "So I'm going to party by myself." Party might be the wrong word, because all he could think about was the look he'd seen in Penny's eyes this morning. The betrayal.

Now she won't look at me at all.

Not that he could blame her. She'd given him her trust, and he'd crushed it.

"She deserves better," he mumbled.

"I think Penny would beg to differ," Huck said quietly.

He frowned at his friend. "What?"

"Please, you think I didn't know? The way you looked at her, the way she was all happy and smiley lately. That was because of you. She loves you. Has for a while. Besides—" he took a drink of his own liquor "—the way you're glaring holes through Finn right now is a big tip off."

"He can give her what she wants."

"Ooh." Huck shook his head. "So you know what's best for Penny?"

"I know it's not me."

"For being a smart guy, you're a fucking idiot."

"Is that right?"

"Look," Huck said. "I know you have your own shit to work out. I know you control your world with an iron fist, and I know why you think the way you do. We've been friends a long time, man. I get it. But you're messing up right now. Really messing up. You've never been one to ignore the facts."

"I'm acknowledging the facts!" Bass said. "I'm not for Penny. It wouldn't work."

"Why? Because she's Ryder's sister? He'll get over it, especially if you love her. But if you really want her, you have to man up and give up one thing to have her."

He didn't have to ask to know what Huck was referring to. But he told him anyway.

"Control," Huck said. "You have to let her choose. Lay it all out there and let her hold your world in her hands for once."

Bass shook his head. If he laid himself out there, she could deny him, rip him to shreds. After everything he'd done to her, he deserved it.

But for her to walk away, it would leave him...

Empty.

Like he was right now.

He'd done this to himself. *She* hadn't done this to him. This whole time, he'd been fighting against himself, and he might have just fucked up his one chance with the only woman he'd be willing to give up everything for.

"You're a good guy." Huck patted his shoulder and stood. "But either figure your shit out and make this right, or you're going to need a lot more of these." He gently tapped the glass he held. "It's up to you to recover from this."

It hit him like a ton of bricks. Though his mind was drowning in Southern Comfort, he was miserable and lashing out, hating himself. Hating life.

Just like my father...

He closed his eyes for a moment, the irony of how he'd gotten to this place despite his best efforts sinking in. He'd turned into the one man he never wanted to become.

Only Penny hadn't left.

I pushed her away.

Chapter Fifteen

Penny had tried taking a cold shower before going to the rehearsal, but her anger had come back to the surface as soon as she arrived at the rehearsal dinner and saw Bass. She refused to let him know she'd seen him.

She'd been nothing more than an arrangement to him. He'd warned her that he liked control, exercised it in all things. She should have known he'd call it off as soon as she threatened that control.

So now she stood at the rehearsal, smiling and nodding while Finn dished her a few compliments.

They'd made it through the second run through of the rehearsal, and just as everyone was talking about loading up and going back to the BBQ for dinner—which she would have to put on another sunny smile for—Colt stood at the alter and asked for everyone's attention.

"I just wanted to thank everyone for coming tonight. I know that tomorrow is the big day." Colt looked at Jenna,

"And I...I just wanted to tell you all that I've been miserable."

Penny's eyes shot wide, but Colt smiled, and his stare locked on Jenna.

"I've never been good with patience," he said. "And every day since the day you said you'd marry me has been a special kind of misery, sugar. Only because I have to wait." He winked at his bride to be, and water danced along her lashes. But what got Penny was the big, bad rodeo rider getting misty. "Tomorrow, you're finally mine. In every way."

Woots, whistles, and applause rang out.

"Bass, come up here," Colt said. Penny's eyes shot to Sebastian as he walked to the platform. "This guy is my best man. He's the one who talked sense into me when I needed to hear it. Now, Bass has asked for a minute to say a special toast. For the man who helped me make the best decision of my life, I'd give him all day."

Colt stepped down, leaving Bass on display and everyone quiet, waiting.

She held her breath as Bass looked straight at her.

"I'm not even a good man, much less the best." He laughed, but there was nothing humorous about it. "I could tell from the beginning that Colt and Jenna were meant for each other. That kind of trust and commitment is rare, and up until a couple of weeks ago, I thought almost no one would be lucky enough to have it, especially me."

She couldn't swallow. She stared at the dark eyes fixed on her. Something other people were beginning to notice. Including her brother.

"If you love someone, it's worth the risk. Whether it's for two weeks, two years...or forever. But something is better than nothing." He shook his head. "I need *more* than *nothing*."

She cupped a hand over her mouth.

"Hear, hear!" someone shouted, and everyone toasted.

As Bass walked off the platform, people went back to their conversations.

And now Bass was walking toward her.

But Ryder stopped him, and the look in her brother's eyes was a deadly one.

. . .

"What the hell is going on?" Ryder asked.

"I've been seeing Penny," Bass said, figuring he might as well come out and say it.

"What do you mean you've been seeing her?" He blocked Bass's path. The man was large, about the same height as Bass, but built more like a bruiser than any of their other friends. "You mean you've been dating her?"

He paused. He could take the lawyer's way out and argue semantics, but he knew what Ryder was asking, and the answer was—

"Yes."

Ryder's face turned a shade of red reserved for people he was ready to punch or run over with his truck. He ushered Bass into the corner and out of earshot. Not that it stopped everyone from glancing at them.

"You mean you've been fucking her," he growled.

"It's not like that," Sebastian said.

"I know you," Ryder said. "I know what you do with women. I know how you operate."

"Maybe it started out like that. But without me meaning

for it to, without me realizing it was happening, it turned into much more."

Ryder took another step toward him, fists clenched at his side. "Did you hurt her? Use and then abandon her like you do all the other women you see?"

"I didn't use her." But he had abandoned her. Something he was anxious to rectify.

"Bullshit! How long has this been going on?"

"Two weeks."

"Two weeks? For two weeks you've lied to me? Shamed my sister in whatever way your twisted mind felt like and walked around like nothing was going on?"

Ryder was beyond pissed, and Bass had no choice but to take whatever he dished out. He knew this was the consequence.

"I know I fucked up when it came to lying to you. And I know I'm not good enough for her. That's why I broke it off. But I can't take it anymore. I want Penny. I want to be with her—"

"Well you can't have her. She's the sweetest, kindest person in the world. She deserves better than someone who's just going to leave her."

"I'm not going to leave her," he said. "It scares the hell out of me, but I'll stay with her for as long as she'll have me."

Ryder clenched his fists. "You and I both know Penny deserves way better than you. Look me in the eye, all bullshit aside, and tell me you of all people are the best man for her."

Bass stared at his friend. He couldn't deny the facts. Ryder had thrown in reasonable doubt. Was Bass "the best man for her?"

He sensed movement on the sidelines. It was Penny,

making her way to the front of the crowd. He looked at her as he said, "I'm not the best man, but I'm damn sure going to try to be."

A searing jab split through Sebastian's cheek, and it felt like his eye was going to explode. Shocking gasps rang out, and it was when the slow burn of pain set in that he realized Ryder had punched him in the face.

"I can't be your wingman on this one, man," Ryder said. He glanced at his sister, then back at Bass. "You want this, you tell her yourself."

. . .

Everyone parted like the Red Sea as Penny made her way to Bass. She hadn't heard everything he'd said, but it had been enough to make Ryder deck him.

She'd tried to prepare herself for this encounter, but it hurt just looking at him. They would never be more. He'd made that clear. So whatever half declaration he'd just made didn't make sense. Because at this point, she didn't know if they could even be friends.

"Penelope," he said, taking her hand and sitting up.

She didn't say anything. Couldn't. Because just the way he said her name made her tremble with anticipation. "Not today."

It was all she could get out. With her friends and her brother looking on, she couldn't go into all this. Couldn't bear to hear his well thought out plan of how to move forward from this as buddies or whatever. She just couldn't.

"Then I'll wait," he said.

Penny frowned, her gaze shooting to his. "What?"

"I'm on your time, Penny."

She took a deep breath, and her spinning world finally slowed, but she couldn't gain her bearings. There, in front of their friends, strangers, and God himself, Sebastian Strafford had done the one thing she'd never seen him do.

He hit his knees.

She opened her mouth, or maybe it fell open, but nothing came out.

"Penny," he said, looking up at her. "I'm sorry."

She shook her head. "What you said this morning..." Just thinking those words hurt.

No. They'd never be more.

"I made a mistake, love," he said. "I pushed you away on purpose. I'm not the perfect guy for you, but I want to try. I love you."

Did she hear that right? There was too much coming at her. The pain of his words, his actions from this morning, and now this declaration that stood in the face of how he'd hurt her.

"I trusted you."

"I know." His arm moved like he was going to reach for her, but he stopped short of touching her. "I messed up. Said things I didn't mean. I pushed you away on purpose." His dark eyes met hers. She saw uncertainty and fear there. She also saw a spark of something else. Love maybe? "I thought you deserved more than what I was willing to give you. I know what you want now. And I want to give you everything. Starting with my control. I'm in your hands now. Whatever you want, I'll do. In return, all I want is you."

Her heart was going to explode, and her whole stomach tightened with pain...with hope. Bass was giving up the one thing he never let go of. Was putting her above everything.

"All I want is you, too," she whispered. Yet there was one thing she had to ask. "How long?"

"What?" he asked.

She gathered her strength and repeated, "How. Long?" It took all the effort she had to get those two words out. But she needed to be clear this time. "You put a timeline on us. Two weeks—"

"*Or* until you say no," he cut in. "I was stupid to think two weeks would ever suffice. It's not enough. Not even in the realm of enough."

His gaze fastened on hers. She saw him, the real Sebastian Strafford and all the raw intensity that came with him. Everything in her soul recognized him as hers.

Suddenly, there was only one question left. The same question she'd asked the first night they started down this path: "What if I never say no?"

Relief and fierce need spread over Sebastian so acutely Penny could see it.

"Then I'll be with you forever." He stood and wrapped her up in his arms, kissing her hard and clutching her close. "I'm so sorry," he said between kisses. "I'm so sorry." He cupped her face, wiping tears away. "I can't be without you. It's fucking terrifying, but I'd rather hold on while I can."

"I'm not going anywhere," she said and hugged him close. "Never."

The way he clung to her, she felt his struggle, and she loved him so much for trying. For her.

From behind them, Huck said, "Do we clap or…"

Penny laughed, and Bass smiled.

"Yes, we totally clap," Colt said. With that, the entire room broke into applause.

They both turned to face their friends. Jenna was beaming ear to ear and all but bouncing up and down. Lily, Huck, and Colt were smiling.

"Well!" Huck said loudly, and then chugged the rest of his drink. "Let's get all this love and shit into gear, because I hear there's a wedding happening tomorrow and a hell of dinner to eat tonight."

With small laughs and sighs, everyone disbursed.

"Oh, Penny," Jenna said. "Will you come up to the bridal suite real quick before we go to try on your dress?"

The bride and bridesmaids were supposed to stay the night after the dinner tonight. Between the rehearsal to the BBQ, then going back to the hotel, it was going to be a long night, but it was worth it to make the bride happy.

"I'll be right up," she called to Jenna and Lily.

When they were gone, Penny was finally alone for a moment with Sebastian in her arms.

"Now, about that the long term arrangement," he said, delivering a quick kiss to her chin. "I was hoping to negotiate terms."

She stepped back and crossed her arms with a huff. "And what terms are those? A three month trial period to reevaluate after a performance review?"

"No," he said. "I was thinking more along the lines of forever."

She gasped, but Sebastian was right there to kiss her gasp away.

There, wrapped in his arms, she'd finally caught the one dream she'd been chasing. Her prince charming and her happily ever after.

Epilogue

"Jesus—" Sebastian said when two small hands reached out from the coat closet and yanked him in. He smiled when he saw Penny standing in the shadows in her fluffy pink bridesmaid gown. "You know, for being a tiny little thing, you sure are strong," he said. The various sweaters and jackets wrapped around him as he moved toward the woman he loved.

Loved.

It was a word he was still getting used to, but he liked the sound of it.

"I can be quite spry when I'm on a mission," she said, smiling.

Oh, he knew that was true.

"We're supposed to be heading back to the BBQ for dinner," he said, just as her back hit the wall and he cupped her hips.

"Yeah, I just wanted to show you my dress real quick." She fiddled with his tie, then looked up at him. "Colt and Jenna will start to wonder where we are. So we better make this quick, counselor."

He didn't need any more convincing. He'd take Penny any way, any how he could get her. Plus, he'd never done it in a coat closet before. Plus.

She kissed him hard, all that passion and need poured from her, and he drank it down. Every touch and taste of her was like a silent plea that she needed him. Wanted him. Would never leave him. And he was a goner for the woman. He was in too deep to ever get out.

Once he'd thought he liked control, but now it was apparent that while he exercised his kinky side, Penny was the one who held his entire world in her hands. And he'd do anything she asked. Hell, all she had to do was make a demand and he'd say, "Yes, ma'am."

And he was totally fine with that.

He delved his tongue into her mouth, tasting sweet strawberries and groaning from the way her lips worked against his. She was growing in confidence. Made him feel like a man worth hanging on to.

She unfastened his pants and shoved them low on his hips as he fought the layers of fabric on her dress, finally getting to her panties and pushing them aside.

He hoisted her up, and she wrapped her legs around his waist. She reached between them and grabbed his hard cock.

He hissed. "Damn it, I want you so much."

She smiled and positioned him at her entrance. "Then take me."

He did. Sliding home, he was greeted with her hot sheath. She was slick and ready, and he hadn't even prepped her.

"You're pretty wet, darlin.'" He thrust again.

She bit her lip. "I may have been preparing myself while

waiting for you."

He growled. The thought of her pleasuring herself made his arousal climb even higher. Holding her up and pressing her against the wall, he slowly, deeply, plunged in and out until she was panting on the brink of climax.

"Prove it," he said.

She brought one of her delicate hands to his mouth, and he sucked her first two fingers. His eyes rolled to the back of his head because yep, he tasted her sweetness.

"You're going to make me come already." He all but cursed, because he wasn't ready to let her go.

"Me too." She hugged him close, her lips at the base of his neck, kissing his jaw, his ear, then finally, he felt her tighten around him and they fell over the edge of ecstasy together.

He didn't know if he groaned or screamed her name. But he did know he'd never get enough of this woman.

With a satisfied smile, she slid down his body and readjusted her dress.

"Now, when you walk around the rest of the night, I want you to think of me," she said, the words sounding a little familiar. She kissed him quick on the lips, but she lingered to say, "Every time you move, you'll feel me."

His eyes widened. He'd said something similar to her in past. With that, she slapped his ass, then walked out of the coat closet, tossing him a wink over her shoulder.

A sly smile split his face. Oh yeah, he loved the hell out of that woman. And she'd just issued another challenge.

Thanks to her, the idea of forever was shaping up to be a pretty awesome one.

Game on.

THE END

Acknowledgments

Thank you to Stephen "Thunder" Morgan for being an awesome editor. Thank you to Candy, Katie, Curtis, and the whole Entangled team for working so hard on this book with me. Thank you Jill Marsal for being the best agent and the most incredible person on the planet. Thank you to my wonderful critique partner for all your help, love, and support!

About the Author

National and international bestselling author Joya Ryan
is the author of the Shattered series, which includes *Break
Me Slowly, Possess Me Slowly,* and *Capture Me Slowly*. She
has also written the Sweet Torment series, which includes
Breathe You In and *Only You*. Passionate about both cooking
and dancing (despite not being too skilled at the latter), she
loves spending time at home. Along with her husband and
her two sons, she resides in California.

www.joyaryan.com

Discover the Chasing Love series by Joya Ryan...

CHASING TROUBLE
a *Chasing Love* novel

Kindergarten teacher Jenna Justice has lived her life by the book—right school, right career, right image. Too bad the townsfolk of Diamond, Kansas, have a hard time forgetting that she wasn't born on the right side of the tracks. Away from prying eyes, she allows herself one sizzling, fantasy-filled night with her best friend's bad boy brother, Colt McCade. His fast-and-loose reputation could cost her everything she's worked for, but walking away might cost him more...

Made in the USA
Middletown, DE
01 August 2024

58351002R00106